⤳ DEPARTURE ⤳

and other stories

DEPARTURE

and other stories

HOWARD FAST

PEACE PRESS

Peace Press
3828 Willat Avenue
Culver City, CA 90230

The following stories first appeared in the magazines cited.
"The Gray Ship," "Departure," and "The Little Folk from the
Hills," *Masses and Mainstream;* "The Rickshaw," *New Masses;*
"An Epitaph for Sidney," and "Where Are Your Guns?" *Jewish
Life;* "The Old Wagon," *Woman's Day;* and "Spoil the Child,"
The Saturday Evening Post.

Printed in the United States of America by Peace Press
Typesetting by Freedmen's Organization, Los Angeles
Cover photograph by Ron Tuso

Library of Congress Cataloging in Publication Data
Fast, Howard Melvin, 1914–
        Departure and other stories.
        Reprint of the ed. published by Little, Brown, Boston.
I. Title.
PS3511. A784D4   1980   813'.52   80–23584
ISBN 0–915238–37–3 (pbk.)

To the men of the Abraham Lincoln Brigade

Books by Howard Fast

Contents

Preface

THIS COLLECTION OF short stories was first published thirty-one years ago. The paper of the edition I look at now as I write this is already yellowed with age; and just as the book itself exists from another era, so do the stories represent another time, a time which today has become what a younger generation refers to as "history."

Many of the stories contained in the book were written as much as a decade before the collection itself was published.

This perhaps underlines my own longevity as a writer. It is almost half a century since my first novel was published and a full half century since I wrote my first short story. Since that time, the world has changed again and again, sometimes violently, sometimes subtley. At the time this collection was first published, the Spanish Civil War was still very much part of our lives. It had led directly into World War II. And the veterans of the Spanish Civil War for the most part were still young men. Today most of them are on the edge of becoming old men, and the agonies of the Spanish Republic appear to belong to a very distant past.

The Thirties were still very much with us when this book was published, and indeed a number of the stories in it were written in the Thirties. Yet strangely enough, people who read these stories today feel that they retain vitality and validity and that they had meaning for us. In this I find very high praise indeed, and the fact that the Press Press is willing to bring out this edition confirms a belief I have long held—that a good story will strike a response in almost any epic and in any situation.

The stories about India were written during World War II, about an India that was still a part of the British Empire. Some of these stories were originally published in national mass circulation magazines. They were written in a time when newsstands were loaded with magazines that published short stories. Today such magazines are very few indeed. Other stories in this collection were published originally in left-wing magazines that have ceased to exist and have themselves become a part of history.

The short story is a form I have always loved—a form that seized the imagination of American writers almost at the moment America came into being, and which in our literature has been brought to a high point of perfection. Today, for a professional writer, the practice of short story writing is a luxury or a labor of love. The markets are few and readers are limited. I sincerely hope that this situation will change. We have in American literature a marvelous, perhaps unequalled, heritage of the short story. It should be added to by each generation. The short story, unlike the novel, is so often a true impression, a flash of insight, a way of seeing the world that no other literary form can provide. I myself have never stopped writing stories and hope to continue with the form as long as I function as a writer.

Departure

IN A WAY, it was like I had become old overnight, and I woke up heavy; I woke up like a man suddenly with a family, two kids and a wife, and rent to pay, but I had none of those things, only a feeling that this, for me, was the end of a lot of things, crazy drinking sprees and whoring and foolish bats of one kind or another, all the things that made them grin at me and put up with it, too, whatever it was, the way you put up with a clown. "Clowning," they would say, "that sonovabitch is always clowning." But they didn't mind.

I shaved carefully and thoroughly, and Laurencon, who had a four-year-old girl at home, made some crack about how she did as well but without a blade, just a timeworn inept crack, but an indication that it was nobody's lark, nobody's day of grace. "Go to hell," I told him.

"No offense, Sonny."

"To hell with you, Pop. You can't offend me. My mind to me a kingdom is. Age is no achievement; it's just a passage of time."

The trucks were waiting, but I still dressed slowly and deliberately. For some reason I didn't fully understand, I had a relationship with my clothes, the boots I had won at the bandage raffle, the heavy brown pants, the blue ski jacket, the

black beret. I had never liked my clothes before, but I liked
them now; they seemed to be unusual clothes, and I felt foolish
and sticky and sentimental toward them. I even borrowed a
clothesbrush from Cohen and brushed them off. It was good
for a laugh from everyone who saw me, but I didn't do it for
a laugh.

The whole battery was like that. To see them offhand,
you wouldn't have known, but as I was with my clothes, so each
of them was with one thing or another; and in the thick soup of
dawn, they moved with measure and deliberation, as if they
were counting out steps to a prearranged dance. I try to think
of some of the things that were said, but it was so long ago and
I was young. Words don't stick as well as the scent of the damp
earth, the sound of the truck motors idling, the pale flash of
a spotlight that had overstayed the darkness. These things made
a pattern for memory; I suppose Lossowski was telling us to step
lively and get moving, but I don't remember for sure. I do
remember that the truck we got into was already half-full of
Croats, big, sleepy-eyed, blond men, who grinned at us and
pushed together to give us plenty of room.

Our truck roared into life, and we drove out of the hospital
compound.

"Good-by, Denia," Mac Goldstein said thoughtfully and
respectfully. Then he handed me one across the behind, and
told me, "Nice to go home, huh, kid?"

"Home is where you make it." Parker, an Englishman,
used to say that, and I picked it up. I would pick up a lot of
words and phrases then; maybe that's the way speech grows
when you're a kid. Sometimes, I used them right, but mostly
wrong, I suppose, and it may be that they stand out across all
that bridge of time for that reason. A word, a phrase, or a sen-
tence is flung away, and how are you supposed to remember,

even if you have taken an oath and are up before a formal court of the law? If I were under oath and answering, I don't know but that I'd perjure myself anyway.

How old were you?

I don't know—twenty or twenty-one.

You don't know? Surely you know. Surely you can think back and calculate. You are an intelligent and thoughtful human being.

Am I?

What date was it?

It was the fourteenth of January, or the fifteenth, or the sixteenth. They don't figure a date by a date, you know; the way they figure—when my first-born saw the light, or when I threw a fistful of dirt on the grave of my blessed mother, or when the cow calved, only there were no more cows then, or when the shadow of the church was ragged instead of straight and heat lightning of four colors flashed in the east; but not by a calendar. So I can remember that before we went into the barracks at Valencia, where they all were, the men of all nations, French and Slavs and Croats and Serbs and Germans and yellow-haired Northmen and dark-haired men of the South, the Italians and the Greeks and the Crete men—before we went into the great barracks there, I saw a Spanish girl who was more beautiful than any other girl that lived, slim and with a lissome stride, and she walked past and was gone, but I remember her and that was the day it was, and I have been in love with her ever since but never saw her again.

I remember too the color of the Mediterranean sky that evening when we went down to the boats.

It was the same day?

Well, I think so. It seems to me that it was the same day. You see, I was in love with the girl, and thinking about her, and it seems that I was only in the barracks for a while, because all I remember, aside from the fact that there were many thousands of men there, was that the Greeks were singing a song. I remember that because I always thought what strange people the Greeks are, not like us or the British or the Germans, either, more like the Spaniards, maybe, and they never seemed to grow tired; it was always beginning for them; wherever they were, it was beginning, a very hopeful people. I remember the song because it was a song of love, and I was in love, in a way of speaking, and the sky over the harbor was like that, pink that turned violet and made me want to cry. You know the way guys are; they kept ribbing me because I had stopped clowning; it wasn't fair to them, I should have kept on clowning, but I couldn't; and then when we marched onto the boat, I began to cry; but it was almost dark and nobody noticed.

It was an excellent operation, smooth and without a hitch, just the way the League of Nations and the Congress of the United States and the Reichstag wanted it to be, except that the boats were old and dirty and rusty and nobody was very sure about what kept them afloat. We marched onto our boat and down the steps into the hold. Before we went down into the hold, I looked back at the beautiful city, Valencia, the jewel, the ancient one. How do I recall what I thought then? I was a kid, a tough, hard-boiled, wisecracking kid who would live forever, but I was tenderly in love and my face was wet with tears, and I must have thought profoundly and deeply. Or perhaps I thought of nothing but good-by.

If I thought good-by, it was the way you do when you are very young, and every place you are you will be back again, so dry your tears of sorrow. The French have a good word for it, but there is no word in English that is just right. There was a Welsh miner there from Pittsburgh, who was a captain with the

129th Brigade, who were Yugoslavs, and a hand grenade had torn open his loin, his testicles, his stomach and his legs, yet he was able to walk; and he stood at the edge of the hold, watching the darkening city, the jewel city, the bereaved one, but said nothing. I don't know what his good-by was. There were thirty-five or forty of us who were Americans, and we went down into the cargo hold, a big, empty place at the bottom of the ship, and all around us there was warmth and odor from the men of many nations, the sick, the wounded, the stretcher cases too, and they clamped on the hatches so that not an ounce of light shone through, and the ship put out to sea.

I can tell it as a dream, but not really as a memory. When I lie at night and I am afraid to die, as all men are, except now and then when there is a thing worth dying for, I think of it, and it's like a balm for a troubled soul. But what is memory as against the facts? And, believe it or not, there is no memory for terror, for there in that hold men couldn't breathe or sleep or move, but I do not remember that anyone was afraid. But maybe my memory is poor and because I was a kid, they were good to me, asking me:

"How's it going, kid?"

"Good enough."

"Well, take it easy. Easy does it."

"Look, lay off me. I'm all right."

"Sure, you're all right, kid, you're all right."

But where do you stow your thoughts when your thoughts tell you that the fascists must know, and they will come out in a fat-bellied German battleship and pick off the old tubs like a hunter picks off ducks? The Slavs made a song; they are the loneliest people in the world, and yet they are never lonely the way we are lonely, and when they sing a song there is a memory of all the hurts they knew and their fathers and their grandfathers. I like our songs better. We sang "Digging Our Way to China." Then we sang "There's a Long, Long Trail a-Winding," which is the most beautiful song in the world, and the saddest, too, as I remember, for someone in love and lost of his love. I don't remember anything else of particular importance, and I suppose we slept.

It was seven o'clock in the sunny morning when we arrived at Barcelona, and for some strange reason our arrival there is confused in my mind with all the old newsreel pictures I have seen before then and since of troops coming home by ship and departing too; but really I don't suppose it was too much like that. But there were people on the dock, and I heard afterwards that Negrin was there. I don't remember him, but I remember André Marty; it was the first time I had seen him, and the guys pointed him out.

They had let us up on deck with the sunrise. A submarine was escorting us, and after I saw it, I felt a lot better. I don't remember us talking about anything else but the submarine, even when we entered the bomb-wracked harbor and saw the sunken ships. And the bigness of Barcelona was different from the loveliness of Valencia. We hold Barcelona, so I told it to the nameless girl who had walked past me with such a lissome stride. We hold Barcelona, and, by God, we will hurl the fascist back into the hills of Portugal, and there will be a victory parade in Madrid, and as I march down the Avenue, I will see her and she will recognize me.

You remember well, and you remember badly?

It's that way, I'm sorry, some little things you remember and some big things you forget. I remember a melon rind floating in the water.

By eight o'clock we were all of us disembarked. The trucks for us were drawn right up to the docks, and we climbed into them. They took us to the barracks, which were on top of a hill outside of Barcelona. I don't know what the hill was called, or what was the name of the barracks, but it was a barracks in the old Spanish style, foursquare, with a compound in the center, and there were balconies all around four or five stories high, a place big enough to hold all of us, and we were thousands. There were all the Internationals who were left; there were the men of the nations. Someone—I don't know who it was—but someone said to me:

"Put it in your memory, kid, put it in your heart."

"My heart is full," I said, speaking in Spanish. "My heart is full and flowing over. I don't want to go home. I have no home, I am the homeless one." You say things in another tongue, and they do not sound foolish, as they would in English. Whoever he was, he answered so softly, *"Vamos juntos, vamos juntos—"* And I thought of the thousand and one times I had wanted to go home, whimpered to go home, pleaded to go home, wept to go home, a frightened kid and no soldier, but now I was a soldier and no land to fight for, no people to give me arms and say: Stand here, stand and no further.

They called us out and we filled the balconies and listened to Marty speak. Then Negrin spoke. Then the whole place broke into the "Internationale," in fifteen tongues, and that is a memory, for when had it happened before and when would it happen again? And we were going away; we were leaving Spain, who is like a beautiful woman you love, and we were going away.

It could have only been a day or two later when the thing happened. The fascists had reached Barcelona, you understand, and we had moved up to a place called Cassa d'la Selva. It was the way out; it was the end already, and there were only the Cubans and the Mexicans with us, and we had stayed too long;

we were guests departed but lingering, and we had given away to the Spaniards left behind our guns, our leather belts, our boots, and whatever else was of value. We ate and we slept and we waited, and rumors filled the air; but the strongest of all the rumors was to the effect of Barcelona being handed over to the enemy, the pig with a voice, the dog without even a dog's soul, the fascist; given up and no struggle; handed over and no struggle; a gift for the devil. I lay in the sun, and my love lay beside me. I told someone then that I was in love. With whom? With a Spanish girl whose eyes are like black olives and whose lips are like poppies. They would have been fools to believe me, but we believed anything then. It was my first love and my last.

You remember what you want to remember; a man's past is part of all the past, and everywhere little gates are carefully closed. Only when it is all finished, our way, will we open all the gates. It was two or three or four days after we were there that the big meeting was called in the one theater the town boasted. Seven or eight hundred of us crowded in there, full and overfilled and cloudy with the smoke of our brown-paper cigarettes.

This is it, kid, someone who knew and was on the inside.

He spoke in Spanish, "You men of the Internationals, *amigo de corazon,* you men of the Internationals who are my comrades, my brothers-in-arms, listen to me! We will defend Barcelona to the death! We go back!"

That is also a memory. I cried again; I put my hands over my face and wept, but I haven't wept since then. Through all the rest, I was dry-eyed. No more clowning, and the kid was not a kid any more. Sitting and listening to the speakers, one after another, telling how Barcelona could be held and made a bridgehead for all free men, I made a disposition of myself. Then we went outside into the dry sunlight of Spain.

The people from our land, America of the lovely name, the free land over the mountains and over the sea, went to a carpentry shop, and there some volunteered and others said they would go home. The volunteers would not go home any more. They stayed together, talking and making arrangements for the battery; I didn't have anything to say, and someone asked me:

"What is it, kid, worried?"

"No."

"Take it easy, kid. Nobody is brave."

"I'm not brave," I said. My childhood was over, youth and adolescence and the sprouting of the weed as juices run through its stem, and the wonderful, beautiful conviction that you will live forever while all other mortals die; manhood is a benediction as well as a curse, and the calm inside of me was life's repayment. It was a fair exchange. "I'm not brave," I said. "I want to stay here."

You see, it was to defend Barcelona to the death, if necessary, and most likely necessary, and you made your own choice. The great bulk of the Internationals were gone, but you had stayed with the leave-taking. You had overstayed; then sleep, and tomorrow we will break bread again.

What else do you remember?

Well, then, I also remember these things: the children who played in the streets, they the inheritors, and I was grown now and saw them as children. The fresh-baked bread we had for our dinner—oh, honored guests. We shared our bread with the children, who made us at home as you do when a guest is no longer a stranger. There were also things to be done, arrangements for the new guns, which were coming down from France, arrangements for officers and for a table of organization, arrangements into the sunset, the sweet, cool night. I was bedded with a cobbler's family, and we sat before bed with a glass of wine and a piece of sausage.

Partake, oh cousin, and tell us about how it goes in the South. Is there death in the South? Will there be victory or defeat? Will the fascists be driven back?

A su tiempo.

Cunning words from an old fighter. You are one of the new ones, a machine gunner?

An artilleryman.

Drink the wine and don't spare the sausage. When will Spain see better men? A glass of wine makes the couch easy.

And then I slept until a whistle wakened me, and this was it, was it not? We formed into ranks and then onto the train, and nobody really knew except—rumors; but after a while we understood. The train was going north, not south. Barcelona would not be held; the last of the Internationals were going away. This was a night train for the border, salute and farewell. Somewhere, men were afraid; somewhere men lost heart and hope, and they had opened the doors and said: Take this maiden for yourself, she with the lips as red as poppies and the lissome stride. I had only hatred and contempt for those whose eyes were wet now.

"What is it, kid?"

"To hell with you! To hell with you!"

And when the train stopped in the morning, we were in France.

The Old Wagon

ON THE SEAT of the wagon, as it drove into the little town, were a man and woman, and a child of six. The man drove two jaded horses; the child, sitting between the man and woman, twisted his head from left to right with never flagging interest. The woman, who was small, sat primly in the seat, as if she knew what a poor impression the wagon made, and desired to counteract it.

The old wagon was piled high with household goods, with pots and pans and chests and chairs and quilts, with much that was no better than junk. Over all, a patched canvas cover was drawn. Roped onto the side were two water barrels. And in back, with bare, dusty legs hanging over the tailboard, were two more children, a boy of eleven, a girl of nine.

The horses were tired, and they walked into the town slowly. The man was tired, and he slouched over his reins, a long, rawboned man with a stubble of beard on his face. Only the woman seemed as fresh as if she had just got out of bed and washed and dressed. She was a little woman, and she sat primly, with her hands folded in her lap. She wore a plain blue cotton dress that fell to her ankles, a duller blue than the color of her eyes, which were large and round and warm. The eyes were the one prominent feature in her small plain face. Her black hair was drawn back tightly under a black bonnet.

It was a few hours past midday, hot, sunny, when they drove into the town. The town consisted of one long street, carpeted with dust, and at this hour it was empty, except for a dozen or so horses standing in front of two saloons.

Briefly, the woman glanced at the town, at the flat house fronts, at the saloons and the horses, after which she folded her hands again a little more firmly in her lap. Her lips compressed, and a click of her tongue told her husband she didn't like the town.

"Don't like it much myself," he admitted. "Got a name for being bad."

"Just shiftless, looks to me," she said. "Now don't stop, but go right through."

"Now, Martha," he complained, "I got to rest the horses."

"Rest them plenty tonight."

He pointed ahead to where the single street of the village lost itself in flat land that was brown and yellow, hot and baked. "How do I know there's water out along there, Martha?"

"You don't know. But if we're a goin' to live there, there's water. That's all."

The child said: "Maw, I'm thirsty."

"See," the man said. "Ain't no reason why the little shaver shouldn't have a nice cool cup of water."

"No reason except that a saloon's the place you'll look for it."

"Martha, there's a trough out there, an' you can't drive dry, tired horses past water without giving them to drink."

"All right," she nodded.

The team scented the water and quickened their pace. They found the trough themselves and plunged their dusty heads into it. The man sighed. The woman clicked her tongue and looked straight ahead of her. The boy began to climb down from the seat.

"You stay here," she ordered.

"Maw, I want a drink."

"Stay here."

"Suppose I get the little shaver a cup of cool water," the man suggested.

"We ain't got money to throw away."

"Now, Martha, why talk that way. I took a pledge nine month past, an' I ain't broken it."

She looked at him a moment. "Guess I shouldn't a said that, Jim."

Awkwardly, stretching his cramped legs, the man climbed down from the wagon. He drew himself up to his full height, worked his neck. Then he ambled behind the wagon and ordered the boy and girl to stay where they were. He came back and patted the horses, and the woman looked at him fondly. He grinned at her, and said:

"Maybe this here's where our luck turns, Martha. Seems we had just about enough bad luck to last folks a lifetime."

"You go get that water."

As he turned to the saloon, the door opened, and two men came out—one short, bowlegged, small of face, wearing blue jeans, booted; the other larger, heavier, better dressed. Both were armed. Both grinned as they looked at the heavily loaded wagon. They came down the steps and stood by the water trough, grinning.

The shorter one said: "Mister, that's a fine load you're packing there."

The other one: "Mister, you buying junk or selling it?"

The woman stared straight ahead of her. If any change came over her face, it was a tightening of her lips, a finer etching of the little lines of pain, of hope, of anxiety about her mouth.

From the shorter one: "Mister, them nags of yours had just about enough water, wouldn't you say? You don't want them to drink the trough dry."

"Jim—" She left off her words and still looked straight ahead of her.

"I never yet been begrudged water," he muttered, shifting uneasily from foot to foot, conscious of the old, patched wagon, conscious of his dirty brown overalls.

"Maybe we begrudge a lot of things to your kind," the taller man said. "Maybe we don't like your kind nice enough to be perlite. Maybe this is cattle country an' not for ground-scrapers."

She saw the stiffening of her husband's body, and she said, quickly: "Jim, we got to get goin'."

"I'll get the shaver a drink of water," he said softly. Then he walked up the wooden steps into the saloon. The two men glanced after him, turned slowly, and followed.

She waited, and it seemed to her that she waited a long time, but actually it couldn't have been more than four or five minutes. Further up the street and across from her was a sign which said CLOVER CITY EXPRESS. It hung over the front of a store, and now, as she watched, a man stepped into the street, and stood under the sign, mopping his brow, a short, stout man in his vest and shirt sleeves. He looked up the street, and then down at the wagon. He met her eyes and nodded.

She felt cold, in spite of the heat. She felt an ominous uncertainty, as before a thunderstorm.

"I'm thirsty," the boy said again.

She heard her husband's voice from behind the saloon door. She unclasped her hands, and they were clammy with sweat. She climbed down from the wagon, instructing the boy,

"Sit there—don't you stir." Walking around the wagon, she saw the boy and girl on the tailboard, leaning back and half-asleep. The girl smiled at her, drowsily.

Then she made up her mind and went into the saloon.

A big place, almost empty, tables and a high, raftered roof, a long bar. She stood just inside the door, her heart throbbing, her hands wet, afraid for herself, afraid for her husband, remembering how he had grinned and told her that their hard luck was broken. She recalled the stretch of their hard luck, the child dying, her husband breaking his leg, the farm taken away from them, their long, painful journey westward.

Her husband stood at the bar. There were about a dozen men at the bar now, men in jeans, booted, armed, their hats tilted back, men somehow different from her husband. At first, she couldn't understand the difference, why it made her afraid; then she realized that they were not men who had ever worked with their hands for a living, not farmers, not cowpunchers.

Her husband was saying: "I came for a cup of water, an' I aim to get it."

The bartender was polishing glasses, ignoring him.

"Jim," she said, "come along."

One of the men said: "Come in, sister. Have a drink."

She saw her husband turn, walk to the man. "That's my wife," he said.

"Sure. I aim to buy her a drink."

"That's my wife you're speaking about."

"Jim!"

She saw his long brown form unlash, saw the booted, armed man sprawl across the room, crash into a table and chairs. She screamed. Her husband didn't move as the fallen man fired. Then, slowly, he bent over, held the bar for support. It had all happened too quickly; it was over, and it was like a dream, like something that had never been. Her husband was bent painfully, holding onto the bar. The others, the booted men, the bartender, were watching. They hadn't moved; they were watching, calmly, curiously. The fallen man picked himself up.

She ran to her husband, and he twisted his head to look down at her. She put her arm around him. "You're not hurt," she said. "Jim, you're not hurt—"

"Maybe—a little."

The others hadn't moved. They were still watching, calmly. She looked at them, started to speak, then clamped her mouth shut. Her hand was wet with blood.

"I'll help you outside," she told her husband.

"All right, Martha."

He leaned on her heavily, and they went through the door. None of the men moved. She shouldered the door open, helped her husband through.

"Looks like our luck kinda run out again, Martha," the man said.

There were people in the street now, a little crowd in front of the saloon around the wagon. The children were standing by the wagon, wide-eyed, excited. When she saw her mother and father come out, the girl began to cry.

She paused on the steps, her husband heavier now, as if all his weight was leaning on her. She felt his blood on her hands. She stood there, feeling his weight, feeling weak, sick, looking at the people around the wagon.

"Some of you—help me," she cried.

They watched her, but nobody moved. She heard the door of the saloon open, and realized that the men inside were coming out.

One man detached himself from the crowd and came up to her. She recognized the stout man she had seen on the street before. He nodded to her, and without speaking put an arm around Jim's waist. They went down the steps, and the three children edged up, shyly, the girl still crying. The people made way for them.

"You can't put him in the wagon, missus," the stout man said. "Take him to my place."

She looked at him, gained confidence from his fat, mustached face, and nodded. They went toward the shop. The children followed. The team walked slowly after them.

From the saloon to the door of the Clover City Express, a trail of blood was left. The children walked in it; the team walked in it, and the old wagon rattled after. The six-year-old was crying now, but through his tears his wide, curious eyes continued to gather everything in. They came to the door of the shop, and when the children stopped, the team stopped too, more satisfied not to move in the hot sun. Some of the bystanders had followed, and now they stood on the side of the wagon where there was some shade, peering into the shop. Two of the men from the saloon stood across the street.

Inside the shop, the woman and the fat man had stretched Jim on a bench. The woman unbuttoned his shirt, bared his breast, and wiped away the blood. His eyes were open, and he tried to smile at her.

"I guess I should a kept the pledge an' not gone near the saloon," he whispered.

"You'll be all right, Jim. You're not hurt bad."

"Where're the kids?"

"Outside."

"That's good. It ain't nice they should see this. What kind a place is this?"

"A newspaper shop, I guess." She glanced around, at the racks of type, at the presses, at the wet proof sheets hanging from a line.

"My shop," the fat man said. "You'll be all right, mister. I'm going for Doc." He nodded at the woman, and went out. She glanced after him, saw the wagon, the children crouched close to it, the bystanders, and across the street, the two armed men from the saloon, standing close to the wall, rolling cigarettes.

When she turned to her husband again, his eyes were closed. He breathed through slightly parted lips, slowly, with effort. She made a pack of cloth over his wound, smoothed back his hair. She looked at him out of her strangely mild blue eyes, and there was no sign of sorrow on her face except the little etched lines of pain about her lips.

She shook her head and went to the door. The bystanders watched her as she came out of the shop. The six-year-old ran to her and buried his face in her skirt. The other two children stood by the wagon, their frightened faces lifted to hers.

"Now, now," she said, "it's all right—you understand? Your pa's just a little hurt, but he's all right." With surprising strength for so small a woman, she lifted the six-year-old onto the wagon seat. "Now you stay there, out of the sun." She turned and saw that the bystanders had drifted away. The two men from the saloon had crossed the street and were standing near the wagon.

"What do you want?" she demanded of them.

"Nothin', missus—only that's a pretty boy you got a settin' up there, a hell of a pretty boy."

Slowly, softly, she said: "I'm not a person to hate. I'm not a person to hold bitterness. What you done, you done. Now get away from here."

"Sure, missus, that's what we like to hear, an' maybe we won't hold no grievance either. Only we were thinking maybe you didn't see nobody shoot your man. Maybe there didn't anybody shoot him, an' it was just an accident. Maybe you could make up your mind that it was an accident because that's one hell of a pretty little boy you got up there."

She turned to glance at the child, and then back to the two men, who were puffing on their cigarettes, their hats tilted back on their heads.

"Get out of here," she whispered.

"Sure, missus. That's a right pretty kid."

"Get out of here!"

They strolled away. The girl and boy pressed close to her, but she seemed hardly to notice them, staring straight ahead of her at nothing.

"You get into the wagon, both of you," she said. "A body's got trouble enough. You get into the wagon an' mind your brother."

She went back into the store, and sat down by her husband. She made a fan of some old newspaper, and waved it over him to cool him. He still lay with his eyes closed. She was sitting like that when the fat man returned with the doctor. The doctor was an elderly man; thin, unshaven, he had a white mustache and a small white beard.

"This is the doctor, ma'am," the fat man said. "I don't know your name; mine's Jed Logan. This is Doc Hartly. He'll see to your husband."

The doctor nodded, took off his jacket, and started to roll up his sleeves. He had small gray eyes that darted from her to her husband.

She rose and turned to the doctor. "My name's Martha Wesley. That's my husband, Jim. I guess he's hurt bad."

"Maybe he is an' maybe he ain't," the doctor said. "There ain't no use thinkin' he is—yet."

"Thank you. We don't have much money, but I guess I can pay what you ask."

"I ain't askin' yet." He opened his bag and bent over the wounded man. Logan took her arm and led her to the back of the shop, through to a little room that held a cot bed, a table and a few chairs.

"Sit down," he told her. "you sit down and rest. I guess you need some rest. I'll fix you a cup of coffee."

"Thank you," she whispered.

"Sure. Sometimes, there's nothing I like much as a cup of coffee, hot as the weather is."

There was a coffeepot warming on the stove. He poured a cup of coffee and set it in front of her.

"Thank you. You've been good to me."

"I'm sort of making up for the way our town treated you, I suppose. Clover City's an up-and-coming place, but a little strange, a little strange."

She drank the coffee. It was good, warm; in spite of the heat, she was cold inside. She liked the fat man who sat across from her. She wanted to like someone, not to feel completely in terror of the place.

"Why did they shoot him?" she asked. "Why?"

"They've shot others, ma'am. They've thieved and murdered."

"But why?"

"Because they're bad, ma'am. Because they're strong, and here, on the edge of things, strength counts. Because there's no law here yet, except the law of the gun, and they've got the guns."

"Aren't there decent people here, men with wives and

children?''

"Sure," the fat man nodded. "I'm decent sometimes, so is Doc. There are plenty of small dirt farmers, small cattlemen. But they're afraid. We're all afraid. They were even afraid to help you with your man."

"You weren't," she said.

"No—" The fat man leaned back and looked at the ceiling. "I got no wife, I got no kids. I'm a used-up newspaperman and Doc's a used-up medico. I've seen it coming, and I'm beginning to talk back. It's a pity I'm not a fighting man, Mrs. Wesley, but I can set type. If you can tell me who shot your husband . . .?''

"I don't know his name." She was thinking of the six-year-old, sitting on the wagon seat.

"You know what he looks like. If you describe him?"

She moved back from the table, folded her hands in her lap. Her wide blue eyes were fixed on the fat man. "They threatened my son," she said. "I have three children. My man's shot—"

"You're afraid."

"I'm not afraid. We've had a lot of hard luck, maybe too much. I've learned not to hate. If my man lives, I'll thank God."

"And if he doesn't live?"

"Then I'll thank God he spared me my children."

"And you love him?"

Her mild blue eyes fixed on the fat man's face. "Why should you ask me that?'' she demanded gently. "Maybe I never told him, maybe he never told me. We're plain folks, an' that kind of talk don't come easy. We been through a lot together. We lost our first boy, fourteen, he'd be now. We lost our farm. It ain't easy, pushing west like this in an old wagon, trying to feed three kids, trying to find a piece of land to light on.''

The fat man said earnestly: "I know that, but this is the kind of West you're pushing into, and this is the kind of thing that has to be stopped. I don't delude myself on the power of my press, still I put out a newspaper, and people read it. If I could print the story with proof of who shot your husband, the governor might read it. It might change things.''

She shook her head. "It might kill my child. I don't want more trouble, mister. I want peace. I want to raise my children in peace.''

The fat man shrugged his shoulders.

"All right, Mrs. Wesley. I hope to God your husband will be all right.''

They went back into the shop. The doctor has evidently finished. He was rolling down his sleeves, buttoning them. The boy and the girl had come into the shop, and were standing in awed silence by the type case. Her husband still lay on the bench, his eyes closed. He seemed to be sleeping.

The fat man and the little woman stood and waited. The doctor crawled into his jacket, closed his bag of tools. He turned to them, then, and said:

"He'll be all right.''

She wavered a bit, nodded, came forward and stood looking down at her husband.

"He's sleeping," the doctor explained. "I gave him something to make him sleep. That's what he needs most now. The wound's nasty, but it ain't bad. Nothing comes of it, and he'll be up and walking tomorrow. It's nasty, but it looks worse than it is. Through the *pectoralis major*, out and through the *triceps*. No bullet to worry about, no organs. But he can't stay here. Suppose Jed and me, we carry him over to my place.''

She shook her head. "You've done so much already—"

"Done nothing. You sit here and read the papers, and we'll be back."

After they had gone, carrying her husband, she sat on a chair near a press, smiling a little. The boy and the girl came and pressed close to her. Then she put her arms around them. She seemed lost in the wonder of having her husband's life again, and at least ten minutes went by before she remembered the six-year-old.

"Where's Billy?" she asked them.

"He was settin' on the wagon seat, sleepin', I guess."

She went outside, and the boy and girl followed. The wagon seat was empty. As in a daze, she walked round and round the wagon, looking inside from the back, lifting the brown canvas cover at the sides. She called: "Billy! Billy!" Her voice sounded strange in the almost empty sunbaked street. Then she stopped walking, leaned against the wagon, limp, tired, staring at the two children who were left.

It was later in the afternoon now; shadows were longer. The little town appeared to be waking up. There were more horses at the hitching posts.

"We left him on the wagon seat," the girl said. The girl was frightened now, ready to cry again.

The mother nodded, and pointed to the shop. "You go in there," she told them. "Lord knows, I got enough trouble. You go in there and stay in there."

"Where's Billy?"

"You never mind that. You go in there and stay in there."

She leaned against the wagon until they had gone into the newspaper shop. Then she sighed, straightened up her small form. The little, etched lines of pain appeared around her mouth again. She walked to the wagon seat, reached under it, and took out a double-barreled shotgun. It was heavy, and she held it awkwardly.

Holding it waist high, muzzles presented, she walked down the street to the saloon. In front of the saloon, she cocked both triggers. Some men, riders, were standing on the porch of the saloon, but when they saw the gun, the look on her face, they made way for her.

"Careful about that popgun, sister," one said.

Another began to laugh, then allowed the laugh to die in his throat.

She shouldered her way through the door, stepped to one side, and stood with her back against the wall. There were more men at the bar now, men at the tables, playing cards. The man who had shot her husband was there. The tall man and the short man were there. The bartender was polishing glasses, and when he saw her, he went on polishing, more and more slowly, his eyes never leaving the shotgun. One by one, they stopped drinking, stopped playing, until every man in the saloon was staring, not so much at her as at the shotgun.

"Is this a ladies' raid?" someone asked.

The short man laughed; the laughter spread, then stopped as abruptly as it had started. The man who had shot her husband took a step forward, hesitated, then another step, then stopped.

"What's your game, lady?" he inquired.

Her voice trembled a little as she spoke. "You took my boy. I came for him."

The bartender said: "Nobody took your kid, lady. Nobody seen your kid. This ain't no place for you, an' you'd better get out a here afore that gun goes off."

"I came for my boy."

Another step forward; his hand felt for his gun, closed

over it.

"Don't come nearer," she said. "You wouldn't shoot a woman, and if you did, this shotgun might go off. I came for my boy. I'll wait five minutes for you to bring him to me."

The bartender pleaded: "Lady, we ain't got the kid."

The man who had shot her husband stared into her wide blue eyes, shrugged, nodded. In a whisper, he said something to the short man, who walked toward the back of the saloon. The shotgun was becoming heavier, and she thought that in a little while the weight of it would be too much for her to bear. Two minutes or five minutes; the short man returned, leading the six-year-old. The child was crying.

"Stop that crying," she said. She dropped the muzzle of the gun, and the bartender sighed and lowered the glass he was polishing. She took the child's hand. "Stop that crying," she said again. Together, they went out.

When she came to the newspaper shop, the fat man and the doctor were already there and waiting. She let the shotgun fall to the floor, dropped into a chair, and gathered the six-year-old in her arms. The doctor picked up the shotgun; the fat man stared at her, a curious expression on his face.

"It's all right," she whispered. "the gun's not loaded."

"They took the kid," the fat man said.

"They took him."

"My God," the fat man whispered, "my God."

She rocked the child back and forth, pressed her face to his until he had stopped crying. The fat man went into the back room and returned with a handful of lump sugar, which he divided among the three children.

"My God," he said again.

The doctor stood there, still holding the shotgun. Outside, the sun was setting. The shadows were longer, blurred. The doctor said:

"I feel young. Young and crazy. I feel like going out there—"

"You're not afraid," the fat man said. "You'll tell me who he was."

"I'll tell you," she nodded, and then she went on to describe the man who had shot her husband.

"That's Rockly. The little one's Krane. God, I'll make something of this. I'll go to the governor. I'll go to Washington, if I have to. I'll plaster the *Clover City Expresss* all over the country. This place is hell, but hell's been changed before. This will start the break. I'll get the extra out tonight."

"They won't let you," the doctor said. "They'll come here."

"Then we'll fight them. It might as well come to that."

"Who? They're all afraid. You're no fighting man. Neither am I. I wish to God I was. I feel young—young and crazy."

"Get them here, Jones, Frisbee, Anlee, Forster. Maybe you can get Clemens and Angus. Get someone to ride for Kenly and Stevens. Get Mat Wythe, Gil Smith. That'll be enough."

"I tell you, they're afraid."

"So am I. She'll talk to them. Get them here and let them look at her. Meanwhile, I'll set type."

"All right," the doctor whispered, "all right."

She sat with her children around her, while the fat man set type furiously. She sat there while the shadows grew longer, disappeared in the haze of dusk. She sat there while armed, serious-faced men entered the shop, spoke in whispers to the fat man, leaned against the wall, holding their rifles.

When they were all there, she spoke to them, and they looked into her wide, mild blue eyes. When she had finished speaking, the doctor took her hand and said:

"Better go to my house now, with the kids. Some of the women are there. Maybe you can help them." He walked with her to his house, leading the team. At the house, he stood a moment, looking at her.

"Good night," he said. "Your husband will be all right." He hesitated, holding her hand. "Funny place, this town. I'd like to see it ten, fifteen years from now. Sometimes, I wish I was younger, sometimes, I don't." Then he turned away, and she looked after him until he had vanished in the night.

She entered the house. As she closed the door behind her, she heard the first shot—after that, many others. That was the beginning of a long, hot tense night—a night that seemed to last forever.

It was early morning. On the seat of the wagon, as it drove out of the little town, were a man and a woman, and a child of six. The man, one arm bandaged to his side, drove two jaded horses; the child, sitting between them, twisted his head from left to right with never flagging interest. The woman, who was small, sat primly in the seat, as if she knew what a poor impression the wagon made, and desired to counteract it.

Almost at the end of the long single street of the town, they passed a fat man standing in front of a print shop. He waved to them. The child stared, wide-eyed, curious. The woman moved slightly, and it seemed that she would wave back; then her folded hands relaxed in her lap, as if she realized that her prim, motionless figure was the only way she could tell the world that the tattered wagon was not the beginning and the end of their life.

The fat man watched the wagon until it became a speck on the brown and yellow plain, until it disappeared.

The Shore Route

WHEN GAXTON GOT himself seated in chair twelve, car one-o-six on the two o'clock train to Boston, he experienced the light-hearted and pleasurable anticipation of someone who is going away on a vacation long overdue. He would get into Boston in four hours and forty-five minutes, all of it on a pleasant, air-conditioned train, and Dick Haley would be waiting for him there, and they would drive out to the Cape together. The Haleys had a comfortable place at Eastham, and for two weeks he would have nothing to do but swim, lie on the sand and get sunburned, and play a little golf if he wanted to.

Even the awkward device of going all the way to Boston to meet Dick Haley, who had some business there, could be construed as an advantage; for the two of them would be in the car for a few hours, and it would enable them to get acquainted again. He had not seen Dick Haley since 1942, and in that time Haley had married and had two children, which makes a difference in any man. Gaxton himself had been married and divorced in that time, except that in between the marriage and divorce were three and a half years in the army. This was his first vacation since he was back, unless you could consider as a vacation those seven weeks after his separation, weeks of getting up the courage to leave his wife and to go back to his old job at Sandrow and Jackson, as a copy writer at six thousand a year.

As a matter of fact, he had looked forward to this vacation all during the latter part of the winter. It wasn't that he was tired or overworked, but rather always expectant of some change that never came. He would have denied that he was lonely or depressed and pointed out, truthfully enough, that he was both optimistic and expectant. Only he was never quite certain about what he was optimistic. After the divorce, he went along from day to day, working—if you called it that—drinking a little, averaging two or three dates with girls during a week, reading a good deal in his little apartment, and dividing the rest of the time between the theater and the movies.

It was a commonplace enough New York existence, and he had often said to himself that he was a commonplace enough New York person, thirty-three years old, rather slim, and not too different from hundreds of others you would see at noon or in the afternoon on Madison or Vanderbilt Avenue. At first, it did not seem possible to him that someone who had been in the infantry through Africa, Sicily and most of Italy could come back to such a commonplace day-to-day existence, but after a while he stopped thinking like that and everything during the war became like a dream. The weeks and months slipped away, and he became expectant. As early as February, he began to think of his vacation, and when Dick Haley wrote to him at the agency asking him to come up to the Cape for the last two weeks of July, he accepted eagerly, and from then on thought about it a great deal.

For all of that, he was rather surprised at his excitement today. Getting on the train, with his golf bag and two-suiter, he felt like a boy off to summer camp, and back of his mind was the foolish refrain that anything could happen during these two weeks.

What the *anything* would be, he didn't know. In the ordinary sense of the word, he had no ambition, neither about his work nor about women. His wife had been a very pretty and intelligent girl, and since he had never fully understood why she had married him, he was not too surprised or shaken when it became someone else in the time he was gone. Gaxton held no real resentment, and once a month or so he would meet his wife for a cocktail, and they would talk very pleasantly about this and that. But he fell in love with no one else—if he had actually ever been in love with her—though he knew enough girls. He was quite good-looking too, but as his wife said to him over one of those cocktails:

"If you would get excited about something—"

He remembered that, because he was excited now at the thought of his vacation. He was excited and expectant and full of anticipation, and the deliciously cool air of the chair car put an edge on his mood. He sat down in number twelve, comfortable and at ease in his seersucker, read his paper until the train started, and then looked around him at his fellow passengers. There were a few old women, the kind you always see on the New Haven, a few businessmen, a family with children, out to vacation, and some young people. One or two of them were nice looking girls, and he considered that after he had his lunch, he might get into a conversation with someone and pass a few hours that way.

His car was the first, directly behind the baggage car, and he had to walk back through two other chair cars to reach the diner. In the diner, the steward put him at a little table by himself. The war was not yet so far past that he could not derive a special kind of enjoyment from a diner, and he lingered over his meal, watching the green, comfortable suburban countryside, and then the endless succession of bays and inlets on the Connecticut coast. He supposed that some day, if he had a family, he would live out here and commute, and he thought idly that it would be nice to have a boat in one of these bays.

He ordered a second pot of coffee, and altogether passed a full hour at the table, and then walked back to his car, stuffing his pipe. But the No Smoking sign caught his eye, and he stood for a moment, irresolute, and trying to decide whether or not to turn back to the club car. Then he recalled that the baggage car was directly in front. He walked through to it. It was almost empty, a dozen suitcases or so, several trunks, and a mass of fresh flowers. At first, he saw the flowers as casually as he saw the suitcases and the trunks, paying them no special heed, except to register in back of his mind somewhere that mostly they seemed to consist of carnations and gladioli, the carnations white and red and the gladioli pink, white, red and lavender.

Striking a match, he puffed his pipe up to a red glow, leaning against the side of the rattling car, savoring the taste of the smoke and feeling very nearly content. Then, a moment later, he realized that the oblong gray box under the flowers was a coffin, and that his companion in the baggage car was some dead person en route to Boston or Providence for burial.

Gaxton was not superstitious, and while in the army his acquaintance with the dead had become rather extensive and more or less intimate. But somehow, he had never seen anything that depressed him so quickly and completely as this nameless coffin. Holding his pipe hard in his teeth, he walked over and looked down at it, feeling that awful curiosity that so many people partake of when they see a closed coffin. He stood there for about five minutes, while pleasure and contentment drained out of him, and then he knocked out his pipe and went back to his seat in the chair car.

But the expectancy was gone. He could see Dick Haley saying to his wife, "You don't mind if I invite Gaxton up for a few weeks. The poor devil's wife walked out on him. You know how it is with some of the men who were in the service."

It was only four o'clock. The two hours and forty-five minutes left before Boston would stretch out forever.

Onion Soup

WHEN THE PURSER, a tall, heavy-set Italian, entered the galley at seven o'clock in the morning, the gray ship was prowling through a fog off the Newfoundland Banks; but there was no sea to speak of, just a gentle swell, and in spite of the stoves, the galley was cold and wet.

The purser looked first at the stock, which had been simmering in a ten-gallon kettle these twenty-four hours past. "How does she ride?" the baker asked. He was a small man with a pocked face, and the purser nodded at him. Six years ago, in the prehistoric past of peace, the purser had been second cook on a fruit boat to the Islands.

"If I was Bill," the baker said, "I would take that little sonovabitch who threw away the carrots and I would put a knowledge of God into him, so help me, I would."

"He didn't mean anything," the purser said, recalling the wrath of the steward when he discovered that the carrots had gone overboard. For weeks and weeks, ever since Sydney, Australia, where he bought them, the steward had husbanded a crate of carrots. Together with two pounds of raisins and a jar of Miracle Whip, they were to make a salad for the steward's dinner. Sometimes, it was hard for the purser to understand how a department, like the steward's could look forward so long and consistently to one dinner.

He thought about that as he watched Bill, the steward,

curse out the messboy. Here they were, so long out from the States that even the memory of the beginning was blurred. From San Pedro on the coast they had gone out to the Hawaiian Islands, from there to Fiji, to New Zealand, to the Solomons, to Iwo, to Australia, and then up the circle to Calcutta; to Ceylon, to Yemen, to Suez—to how many other places? Day in, day out, the stewards put the meals on the table, until, the last day before making port in the States, the order was reversed, and the cooks, bakers, messboys and the others sat down at the table, to be waited on and served and fed. The purser had volunteered to do the cooking, and the carpenter had come on as his second, and a fool of a messboy had thrown out a crate of carrots.

"It is not," the steward said, speaking his slow Texas drawl, "that we can't put on a meal for them. I got three and fifty pounds of *filet mignon* in the box and there's plenty of potatoes to fry. But I was counting on the carrots."

The purser agreed that a salad was nice.

"It's not only that. Sure they can sit down to steak and potatoes. But you eat one meal out of a thousand and you want something special."

"Like what?"

"God knows," the steward said. "But not Jello and not canned peaches. Last week we had apples—fried apple rings. But the apples are gone. The eggs are gone."

"How about onions?" the purser asked. "Because once I ate a Normandy onion soup that was something to dream about."

"Plenty of onions," the steward said without excitement.

He didn't particularly like onion soup.

"This isn't like what you ate. This is out of the world. I only ate it once."

"How do you know you can make it?"

"I like to cook," the purser smiled. "I got a feeling for it. As long as you have plenty of onions."

But actually, it was a long shot, and he didn't know whether he could make the onion soup or not. He had a crate of onions out, and he was peeling them when the carpenter came in, put on an apron, and went at the potatoes.

"Onion soup," the carpenter said, "is bad gravy with onions floating in it."

The purser shook his head. "I come from a people who know food and like food."

"How's that?"

"You know what my mother, she used to tell me when I was a kid? Eat your vegetables, she used to say, because when you grow up and marry an American girl, you'll eat boiled vegetables."

"What's wrong with boiled vegetables?" the carpenter wanted to know.

"Nothing. But food is a mark of civilization. This onion soup is a mark of civilization. In all my life, I ate it only once. That makes me sad."

"It wouldn't made me sad," the carpenter said.

When he had finished peeling the onions, the purser went out on deck. They were not doing more than six or seven knots, and the wind was off shore, and the purser wondered whether he could smell home in it. Yet he was still three thousand miles and more from home and a wife and two children, who were in the San Fernando Valley; it was what would happen to him, he thought, to go out of the West Coast and into the East. For a while, he watched the sluggish gray water, until the third engineer came along and said:

"I hear you're making an onion soup for the stewards."

"So?"

"I ate good onion soup in France but no place else," said the third, a small, dry and melancholy man in his late forties, but only to make conversation, leaning on the rail alongside of the purser. In the purser's home, food was life and life was food, with avocado trees in the front yard and the best paste in all of California, or so he thought and his four brothers and his three sisters and his wife and their wives. The white bread was home-baked and the *manicotti* had once made a poet sing of it. You sat at a table and life rewarded you for having the temerity to live.

"This is a Normandy onion soup," the purser said slowly, apart from the third, born and brought up in the States, but always a stranger to these folk who had no food, only quantity, no love for food, no understanding of food, no relationship to food.

The third shrugged and spat onto the rush of wind, and the purser went back into the galley. "I only ate it once," he said to the carpenter, "and it was golden brown, creamy, and the essence of onions came from it, but never a taste or touch of onions. You get to figure you can make a food, if you know how to cook, even if you don't know just what goes into it."

"I was a short-order cook in a diner in Omaha once," the carpenter said. "I was also cook in a lumber camp for Toohey Brothers back in the old Wobbly days, but what they ate shouldn't happen to a dog. Where did you learn to cook?"

The purser sliced onions and remembered that he was second in the huge galley of the old *America,* and way back in forty, before it properly began, he had shipped on an oiler that later went down on the Murmansk Run. He was first cook, but where had he learned to cook? In a hot, sunny California memory, he watched his mother cook, but the nostalgia of the memory was apart from any curriculum. The onion juice ran over his hands as he brought back the wonder of childhood, adding to it the strange fact of his own children.

"Slice me about five pounds of bacon, thin," he said. And then added, "You don't learn to cook."

The cook and the second cook joined the carpenter and the purser. The ship was a condition of perpetual hunger, and even if this was the day of the steward's department, three meals had to be cooked and served. But a lunch of potato salad and cold cuts and supper of baked macaroni with cheese and ham was recognized and admitted as a bow to the special nature of the day. The top of the long galley stove belonged to the purser and the carpenter, and the cook, a fat, pock-marked mountain of a Greek, and the second cook, yellow-haired and skinny, from southern Oklahoma, both recognized this fact, adopting a deliberate and somewhat mawkish dilettantism. It pleased them that they were strangers in the galley on this day, and having little enough work, what with the cold cuts and the one huge casserole, they snooped around like tourists.

"Onion soup?" the cook asked.

"With *filet mignon* and fried potatoes," the carpenter added. "You won't starve."

"I don't see a potato again in this life, I won't shed no tears," the second cook said.

"But onion soup—" the cook said, and then, fearful that he had hurt the purser's feelings, added, "I got some gallon cans of bouillon if you need it."

"Bouillon," the purser said softly. "Mother of God, bouillon!"

"You leave him alone," the carpenter said. "What in hell are you guys doing here anyway? Take your stinking cold cuts into the pantry. Take them to the head. Here we are slaving away over a hot stove and you got no appreciation, only an interest like a couple of marks in a summer carnival.''

He shouldered them out, and the purser selected a frying pan thirty inches in diameter, laid out the bacon on it, and set it to fry. As the bacon began to sizzle and blister, he mentioned to the carpenter:

''Why do you suppose he ships out as cook?''

''It's a living,'' the carpenter said. ''I'm an old man, but if I was a young feller, I'd learn me to cook. I wouldn't be no deck hand.''

The purser hung over the frying pan, guiding the strips of bacon, lifting out each piece as it browned and laying it on a big sheet of Manila he had spread on the table. As the fat in the pan increased, the remaining strips of bacon danced merrily. It was a long and tedious process, but he carried it through until he had a pan of fresh, bubbling lard, not burned and not smoking, and all of the bacon crisp and browned evenly.

''You going to eat lunch?'' the carpenter wanted to know.

The purser shook his head. For the first time in months, the loneliness, the awful combination of space and time, was falling away. Standing in his shorts, his big, brown, hairy body warmed to the heat of the stove and swayed to the gentle roll of the ship. The onion soup became more than a soup, more and beyond his explaining to anyone.

When the last of the bacon was finished, the purser added salt to the fat and ground down peppercorns, which he spread through it evenly. He set it on a low light and tried to think of spice. After he had eaten the Normandy onion soup, that single time, he had gone in to the cook and asked her. She was a wizened shred of a woman, with blue eyes as pale as the winter sky.

''You make it,'' she said.

"But how—how do you spice it?"

She put her hands on her flat dugs and rocked back and forth, gurgling with laughter. "You go to hell, huh?" she laughed, and then added, *"Tu peux m'embrasser quelque part."*

He went out and told his wife. "That's a nasty old woman," his wife had said. "It's good soup, but I don't see why you make such a fuss about it."

"It's the most wonderful soup a man ever ate."

Now he brooded over the matter, tossed a mental coin finally, took a small sifter, and put a heaping tablespoon of curry powder through it, spreading it evenly over the fat. Then he separated the onions into rings and added them. The mountain of onions fried slowly, the purser perched on a stool and poking at it now and then with a long fork. While he sat there, the carpenter brought him a sandwich, which he munched thoughtfully. He had been sailing for five years now; suppose he came home and found that the war was over? Would he go on sailing? Where do old sailors go? He looked at the carpenter.

An A.B. came in, a lad of twenty-eight or so, nodded at them and then studied the onions. "You got a lot a fat," he said appraisingly.

"I drain it off after a while," the purser said, "and I let it dry out on the pan."

"I hear you're making onion soup," the A.B. remarked.

The purser grinned. "It gets around."

The A.B. stayed until the fat was drained off and the onions nursed back on the pan. "I'll need some bread," the purser said to the carpenter. "About thirty slices. Cut them about half an inch thick, shape them round with a cake cutter or something, and then sprinkle them over with garlic salt. Pack them up like six-decker sandwiches and let them sit." The onions were finished now, and the purser let them simmer on a very low flame. Then he crushed the dry bacon with a pestle and put it in with the onions, mixing it slowly.

"It don't make sense about the bread," the carpenter said. "What in hell's name will you do with it?" Scrunching through the great icebox, he had found two shriveled survivors of the apples they had taken on at Sydney. They hitched up on the table and chewed the apples.

"That's the one thing I know," the purser answered. "There was a slice of toasted bread on the soup, and it was done with the garlic salt, packing it, and letting it soak through. It does it, if the bread is fresh."

"A guy as crazy about food as you," the carpenter said, "he ought to be pretty fat. You're not fat."

"I like good food," said the purser, "but it doesn't depend on how much I eat."

"If a guy likes dames—"

"I got to put that mess through a sieve," the purser sighed. "A ricer wouldn't be any good." The steward came in while they were searching through the cupboards and he found them a huge iron cone, threaded through with holes, like a helm out of the Middle Ages, and he stayed to hold it as the purser pounded through the onions and bacon, which emerged as a purée. Two oilers who had heard about the soup joined the carpenter.

To the purser, one of the oilers said, "I been in Normandy. I never ate onion soup there."

The other had an ache behind his left ear that had been bothering him all day, and since the ship carried no pharmacist's mate, the purser dispensed medicine and sometimes surgery out of three large books. He went to the cabin with the oiler, looked into his ear, looked into the book, and then gave him two aspirin and some sulfa gum to chew. With afternoon, the sun had emerged, and the purser stood on the boat deck for a while, craning his neck to watch them paint and bed down the twenty-millimeter guns. The steward was waiting for him when he returned to the galley. They put the purée into an eight-quart pot and then drew the stock, while the whole galley steamed with the strong smell of twenty pounds of meat, bones and gristle that had thirty hours of cooking behind it.

When the stock was drawn, the purser mixed it slowly and gently. The second mate joined the oiler, and the carpenter, who was opening cans of peaches for dessert, said, "Why don't you taste it?"

"First, the *roux*."

It had become ritualized. A wiper and the first mate added themselves to the crowd, and the steward went to the box and returned with two pounds of butter. Putting it in a pan to melt, the purser began to sift his flour. There was an easiness about them, they had been together so long, but also a tenseness, and the steward could only think, "What a damnfool thing over a pot of soup." But the wiper said stolidly, "I'd use arrowroot."

Nobody laughed. The purser stared at him for a long moment, and the wiper, a dark little man, nodded back solemnly.

"You got arrowroot?" the purser asked the steward.

The steward went for the arrowroot. The purser let the butter brown delicately, and then turned it with the arrowroot, bit by bit; using a big wire whip and thicking the *roux* as he worked. They were silent while the *roux* cooked, and then, when it was ready, they watched him blend it into the soup. There it was, golden brown, almost eight quarts of it.

"Taste it," the steward said.

"It looks right," the purser murmured, a curious expression on his face.

"Go ahead and taste it," someone else said.

The purser tasted it, and it wasn't right, and he thought of the little, dried-up Normandy woman laughing in his face. The others watched him but didn't ask to taste it themselves. He added pepper and salt and tasted it again. The steward raised his brows inquiringly.

"Something's missing," the purser said slowly. They all felt what he felt now.

"You'll get it," the wiper said. "You only ate it once. You want to remember what it tasted like. Maybe that was a long time ago. Just think about the taste."

Now they felt worse than he felt, and there was an element of love as well as sadness as they watched him walk out of the galley onto the deck. "To hell with it, it's just soup," the carpenter thought, but he was sad too.

The purser walked to the after hatch and sat down next to the cook, and for a while the two of them sat silent, watching an ordinary paint over the rust where shrapnel had scored and punctured the rail.

"The son of a bitch," the cook said finally, but the purser said nothing at all, and the Greek guessed what it was. "They can somehow pull through on steak," the cook said. "It will be tough, but they'll pull through."

"It's not that. I feel like I'm coming home empty. It's a crazy way to feel, but that's what I feel."

"I was on a C3," the cook said, "and I had a second who was a Swiss, and he put nutmeg into every soup he made."

"Nutmeg?"

"Nutmeg," the cook said. "Me, I make an onion soup from old gravy. I fry some onions and let them swim. To hell with it—it's onion soup."

"You ever put nutmeg in soup?" the purser asked.

"I beat the ass off that damnfool Swiss once I found out."

"You got any nutmeg?" the purser asked.

"I got a bag of nuts somewhere."

"Let's try it," the purser said.

They went inside, and the cook found the nutmegs. The purser took half a ladle of soup, and the cook scraped the nutmeg into it. Then the purser tasted it. "A little more," he said. He tasted it again, and it was right, like no other soup the world had seen, and then he let the carpenter and the cook taste it, while he thought about the way the old Normandy woman had laughed. The steward wanted to taste it, and so did the wiper and some of the others, but the purser shook his head.

"If any's left over," he told them. "I got to get supper." And he put the garlic bread into the oven to dry out slowly.

That night, the purse stood on deck, arms on the rail, and watched a lighthouse blinking, on and off, on and off. He felt warm and close to a lot of people, and he wanted to cry because he was home and he'd say good-by to them and never see them again. There were twenty-two people in the steward's department, and when the meal was over, one by one they came into the galley where he was washing dishes, and they shook his hand and each of them said something about the soup.

Then the old man sent down for a plate of the soup. The old man was a Dane and fussy about his food and always cursing out the cook, but he sent back for a second plate of soup. He wanted to know how it was made.

"Tell him to go jump in the drink," the carpenter had said.

It was funny, the purser thought, because they were as hard-bitten a group of men on the ship as he had ever known, hard men who were all knotted up with work and too many long trips and too many torpedoes and too many dive bombers and the closeness of a piece of iron where they had been living almost forever. It was funny, he thought.

And he thought of how he would tell his wife about it, and she would not see anything in a pot of onion soup to make all this fuss about. He thought about his wife easily and pleasantly now, and he kept on thinking about her as the blinking light faded into the distance.

An Epitaph for Sidney

WE THOUGHT AT first that an epitaph for Sidney should be more than a few words, and I and some of the others who had known him well set out to collate what information we had; but in the end we did not use the material, and it was handed over to me. From what we have, you will be able to see why we were able to write an epitaph for Sidney in a line.

Some of us knew Sidney Greenspan when we were very young. He was born in the year 1915 in Washington Heights, and he grew up there and went to Public School 46, and then he went to De Witt Clinton High School, and then he went to City College—but he didn't finish at City College. He was a thin, spindle-legged little boy, and he never really achieved height or any sort of muscular efficiency, and since he read a lot and studied a good deal afterwards, he came by myopia early, and it remained with him.

He came from a family of very poor Jews, one of five children, with a thin, tired mother and a father who worked at a sewing machine in one sweatshop and then another; actually, he didn't have to work in sweatshops; he could have worked in union shops, as Sidney told him and pleaded with him, but he had been fifteen months out of work in the long strike during the twenties, and that had taken the starch and the heart out of him and turned him into a piece of putty. The result was that he worked ten and twelve hours a day in sweat-shops, always thinking that if a strike came, it would leave him alone. Sidney's mother, who was like a shadow moving here and there, cooking and cleaning, but always like a shadow, gave to the children and never asked anything in return, not even love, until she died in 1932. Sidney had just entered college when she died. In a letter to a friend of his, he wrote ". . . I don't feel pity or sorrow, only anger. . . ." Mr. Green-span lived on and shriveled up; he went on with his work motions, like an old clock that was winding out, ever more slowly.

Of Sidney's brothers and sisters, only two grew to maturity. One fell under a truck at the age of seven, a little boy named Lester. Celia, the elder sister, died of a mastoid. Adrian and Fannie are still alive; Adrian became a schoolteacher, and the old man, Mr. Greenspan, was most proud of him. Fannie mar-ried a fur worker; she was two years younger than Sidney, and when she was a little girl he adored her.

II

Even in this brief outline, there is enough to indicate that Sidney Greenspan was not of the stuff of which heroes are made, at least in the conception of heroes which is most popular in America today. The tenement district in which he lived and grew was not a slum, but very close to a slum; the fact that he was a small, thin boy gave his life reasonable hazard, in the way of Jew-baiting and the run of fights. He was often afraid, and there was much and subtle variation in the types of fear; he feared death and being beaten up and going hungry and not passing exams, but one fear and another was woven into the fabric of his life and accepted, just as he accepted the fact of work from the age of eleven, first as a delivery boy, then with a newspaper route, then as a canvasser for the local Tammany Club, then as a hack political street-corner speaker at the age of sixteen. His father went around with a bright hope burning in his heart that Sidney would study law, but in the first year at City College, Sidney's jaw was fractured in a student demonstration, and amid reacting to the pain of his son's bruised body, his father realized that the boy was a radical and came to accept the fact that he would not be a lawyer, not an alderman, nor even an assemblyman, not even a schoolteacher.

But fear did not make Sidney a radical. Such cloth is woven of other stuff, and for Sidney there was a world lost that should not have been lost. Some are made or shaped or fashioned to see all the parts of the whole, not one direction or one street or one narrow alley, but all the roads that lead on; and it was for a part of that horizon that Sidney stayed with the class that made him. If he had accepted, his epitaph could have been more easily written, but he didn't accept—he had to understand. In one way, there was a tremendous health and vitality in his small, skinny body, an identification with life that was more than matched chromosomes or cell clinging to cell. Death gives the lie to life, refutes it, and all the misshapen things that Sidney saw were part of that death. And he walked into life with his head up; vitality is a manner of saying other things. The vitality of Sidney made him a prow rather than a rudder.

"I told him," Mr. Greenspan said long afterwards to one of us who knew Sidney, "that it was no good. He would get in trouble, he should try to be a good, hard worker and keep out of trouble."

But Sidney didn't look for trouble. As a boy, he hardly

ever won a fight; he wasn't a tough kid, and he stayed away
from fights whenever he could. He always had a job after school,
and even to go to a free college like C.C.N.Y. he had to work
during the summers. Two summers he worked at Lang's Whole-
sale Grocery Warehouse downtown on Hudson Street, until he
became involved with attempts to organize it and was fired.
And then he had a job one summer at Coney Island, handling
props for a magician's show. But the point is that he never
looked for trouble, and you could see that just by looking
at him.

He didn't look any different at eighteen than he did at
twenty-five, about five feet seven inches in height, a hundred
and thirty-two or -three pounds, with sloping shoulders, a
prominent nose, and thin brown hair. His brown eyes were
reflective and gentle, giving an impression of sympathetic soft-
ness; you were surprised to find something hard and absolutely
unyielding underneath; no matter how long you knew Sidney
you were always surprised at that.

When he was eighteen years old, a freshman at City College, he met Jane Albertson and fell in love with her, in spite
of such obvious obstacles as both her parents having a little
money and being descended from what they call "old American stock," and her being an inch taller than he was. And the
strange part of it was that after the usual initial fumbling and
antagonism she fell in love with him, something nobody understood except those of us who knew Sidney. The first time he
brought her home with him, to the same, tiny apartment
where the Greenspans had always lived, the old man was still
grieving over his wife, with a kind of awful, dumb-animal
suffering. The apartment was dirty and messy; Fannie tried to
keep house, but it was not the kind of thing she was good at,

and Adrian was already married. Janie walked in with the air of a person who had spent most of her life in such places, and she kissed the old man. The old man began to cry, and Janie remembers that Sidney was the most embarrassed one there, and when she said she would stay for supper, he put on his jacket and ran down to buy things in the delicatessen. But after that, Janie and the old man were like a daughter and father.

The way they fell in love and the way they went together all the time Sidney was in college was a little curious, for time was something Sidney never had much of. He clerked in a dry goods store after school; he was active in the student movement; and then in 1934 he joined the Young Communist League. But, somehow, he and Janie were closer and closer. She joined the YCL too, and had some terrible fights with her people at home; and then, in 1935, they were quietly married at City Hall, something they kept a secret for almost four years.

Only a few of us, who knew Sidney quite well, also knew about the marriage. It was in 1934 that I first met Sidney, and I was with him when his head was cracked by a nightstick in the big downtown demonstration, and I got him home then and stayed with him while the doctor came and put seven stitches in his scalp. It was then that Mr. Greenspan, almost tearfully, raised the question:

"Why, why should he have to mix up in such trouble?"

Lying there, Sidney said, "Please, Poppa, don't worry about it."

"A good boy, a boy who works as hard as he does."

"Poppa, I don't look for trouble. You think I like to get cracked over the head?"

"I don't know what to think," Mr. Greenspan said.

"Wherever you look, those Communists make trouble. They got nothing else to do except to make trouble."

"This is such a good world, you want me to accept it?" Sidney said.

He changed after that; they say that no scar is skin deep. When you tell it this way, looking back, with all of us a good deal older, and in retrospect, none of us ever having been very young, it doesn't seem that there was so much in Sidney's life; there is no ABC formula to put your finger on to explain Sidney. He said to me once, I think when he was nineteen years old, "Do you know, I'm a professional revolutionary"— as if it had only occurred to him that moment; but as a matter of fact, it was so, and every other action he engaged in was on the periphery. In those days—it seems a thousand years ago, five histories ago—it seemed that the world we lived in could not go on; and indeed that world is dead today, washed out in the blood of thirty million souls, even if the fight is not over. But someone like Sidney belongs to that world; when there is a perspective, sometime in the future, the long, long future, when the fighting is over, when the guns no longer thunder, when the scars left by the atom bombs have healed, when the gray ships lie peacefully on the ocean bottoms, then there will be a whole understanding of Sidney, of what he was and what went into the making of him. Then, perhaps, they will be able to analyze the trivia as well as the bigger things. They will know what the expression on Sidney's face meant when he heard his father say once, speaking of his not long dead mother. "All she wanted was two weeks in the mountains, with a little grass and some birds, maybe, but she never got that."

But Sidney's hatred—and there must have been a fierce, terrible hatred of the things that pervert and destroy human beings—found expression only in what he did; the mildness in this small, sensitive Jew was so entire that even we who knew him well were surprised when he left college to join the International Brigade in Spain. He hated and mistrusted guns; the most complimentary thing we could say was that a person as politically developed as he might make a very good advisor, or commissar, as they were beginning to call them. But as a matter of fact we were wrong, and after the retreat across the Ebro, they made him a captain.

III

I had the story of the retreat across the Ebro, and the last attack, afterwards, from at least six or seven people who had known Sidney and fought next to him. Also, in his letters to Janie and to old Mr. Greenspan and to Adrian, his brother, and to his sister, Fannie, there were enough details to make some sort of blueprint, but he didn't figure in that blueprint; he wrote of the things all around him, and it was his comrades who filled in the place he occupied.

Remember how it was then, in 1937, when the Lincoln Battalion first raised its banner with the International Brigade! Madrid was to be the tomb of fascism! Boys who had never seen anything more lethal than a cop's revolver signed up for the Battalion; skinny, myopic boys from the city streets marched off alongside the workers to face the Messerschmitts and the Panzers. The final conflict was being fought among the treeless buttes and canyons of Spain, and from the devastation wrought by the first fascist monsters would arise the beginnings of the brave new world. We believed that—and looking back, it might have been that way.

It was early in 1937 that Sidney Greenspan arrived with his contingent in Spain. Between then and April of '38, when the retreat across the Ebro took place, he had two slight wounds; he became a lieutenant, he learned how to assemble a machine gun with his eyes closed, and he learned more thoroughly that if you considered in advance what you were going to do and did it, it was better for body and soul than to straddle the horns of a dilemma. But on the outside, he remained the same; he still studied a good deal. In those days he read everything he could have sent to him on the working class in America, and when he talked about the future, it was with the certainty that this phase of the struggle would soon be over, and he thought he would like to be a labor organizer in the South, going there to live and taking Janie with him.

When the big retreat began in '38, he was with the 58th Lincoln Battalion. But they didn't know that it was a retreat then. It was determined at GHQ that the tide had to be turned, whatever the cost, and Dave Doran, the Brigade Commissar, wrote orders to advance and keep advancing until otherwise instructed. So the 58th Battalion advanced, not knowing that everywhere else the line was breaking and all up and down the long front the battered Republican Army was in retreat. Here is the matter-of-fact way in which Sidney told about that in a letter to Janie:

. . . please don't worry, because I'm all right now. But it was bad a few weeks ago, and we lost most of the Battalion. Maybe you will read about it in the papers, but here is the truth of how it happened. Johnny Gates, our Commissar—you remember, you met him at Milty's house—told us about the general orders to go ahead, and we went ahead and we just kept advancing. First we were low and very thirsty, but we captured a fascist water truck, and we felt better. But we were moving fast with just the ammunition we could pack and we had no liaison and we didn't know that everywhere else our people were retreating. I don't know who was to blame for that; I don't want to blame anyone now.

Well, we went on with our crazy, wild advance until about three o'clock in the afternoon, and then we were resting under some olive trees when we realized something was wrong. Bob Merriman—he was from California U., Brigade Operations Officer—came up and told us to get the devil out. There were about three hundred of us then, I mean boys from home, and we hit out cross country. We got to a hill above Gandesa, and we looked down, and we could see the fascists attacking in the streets, and some of the houses were burning, but our people still held a good part of the town. Merriman thought the wisest thing to do would be to break through to the defenders, and we sent out a patrol of about twenty-five guys. They were wiped out, all of them. It was like the end of something, the first end. We retreated onto two hills, the Americans on one, the Spaniards and others on the other. They sent cavalry against us then, and we repulsed the charge, cutting them up pretty good. Then the cavalry dismounted and set up lines, and along about dusk, they started in with artillery. Then Vernon Selby—he's that boy from Virginia Military Institute— found a way out for us, and it seemed that Corbera was still open.

Here's where we lost all our men, including Spaniards. We went Indian file and traveled at night, across country. Men would go to sleep and not wake up, just out of weariness. They would crawl into the bushes and go to sleep, and we'd lose them. We'd think they were there and go on. How can we forgive ourselves for that? Then we ran smack into Corbera, into a German radio station. They started in with grenades and machine guns, and cut us to pieces. Merriman and Doran were killed there, but I didn't know that then. But that broke us up, and I took off with two other guys, Smith and Goldstein. Somehow, we got to the Ebro. They were both wounded, and the next night we had to crawl through a whole sleeping Italian division. But only sixty of our guys got across the Ebro—only sixty. . . .

Sidney didn't tell her, in that letter, that when Smith and Goldstein were wounded, he had cared for them, nursed them, and sometimes carried them, that he bore them both across the Ebro. He didn't tell her that the next day he recrossed the Ebro and found Abel Clark, and dressed his wounds and returned with him. How he did it and where his strength came from can't easily be told; he belonged to something new and incredible, that came out of the people. For the moment, it can merely be detailed, as an epitaph or as a requiem. He stopped a tank once with a bottle of petrol and a rag, and once he broke his glasses and fought for two weeks in a shadow world.

He was in the nine days on the Sierra Carbolam after they had mounted the last offensive back across the Ebro and had won almost to Gandesa. Then he was a captain—he became a captain after the retreat across the Ebro—and his company hung onto the rocky lump of Hill 366 and then was pushed off it under the fire of heavy artillery, with no other cover than some sandbags and the bare rock. In three days, he led twelve attacks to take back the hill. But afterwards, when he spoke about it once, the thing he mentioned was how, coming back to the lines after a short rest, they met the Dimitroff Battalion, the Slav Battalion; all the boys in the Brigade knew that the Slav Battalion was the best, iron and steel, and not to be broken by anything short of hell: and when the men from the Dimitroff outfit, beat as they were, saw the Lincoln Battallion going up to fill the hole for them, they broke down and wept. The big, blond Slavs stood there, crying, and then they joined the Americans and all of them went up together, with some rifles and some pistols, against the heavy artillery, the armor, and the Junkers-filled sky.

After that, Sidney was not afraid; he would say that he only had to remember that and he wouldn't be afraid. And it was not long after that that he was taken by the Moors. Some of the boys who were there remembered exactly how it had happened. The Battalion thought there was a Spanish outfit on their right flank—good men, not fascists—and a patrol went out. Sidney took the patrol out; Jim Lardner was with

him, and that was where Lardner died, and Sidney was taken
by the Moors.

IV

About the time in prison, Sidney had least to say. A jail
is a jail in any land, and the rats, the mice, the bedbugs, and
the soul-destroying monotony are international qualities. But
the fascists, wherever they are, develop refinements. The Moors
amused themselves by breaking all the fingers in his right
hand, and Sidney thought he would never be able to use it
again. They found out that he was a Jew and they turned him
over to the Nazis. The Nazis, who were more creative even than
the Moors, had developed in Spain the standing cells, which
they were putting to such good purpose against members of the
German underground. A standing cell is two and a half feet
wide and a foot and half deep; you stand in it until your legs
and your mind go, and then you fall, but there is no place for
you to fall. For six weeks they gave Sidney the standing cell
for two days a week; they were scientifically curious about how
much such a small, frail young man could take, and they had
theories about Jewish blood and Jewish powers of resistance,
and it was always interesting to test those theories under actual
conditions.

How Sidney escaped still cannot be told; Franco still sits
like a blood-fatted spider in Spain, and the gentlemen in our
Congress still debate. But he escaped, and he made his way
to the coast, and a small boat took him to France. He was
twenty-four when he came back to America, and his hair was
turning gray, and he didn't care to talk much about how it had
been in prison. His main interest was to find out whether he

could ever use his right hand again, and when the operation turned out successfully, his whole state of mind became better. He and Janie went away for the three months his hand was in a cast; it was the only time Sidney had anything like that, three months in the country, with nothing to do but sit and read and taste the sweetness of life.

He could have gotten a job in a good berth; he had friends; he had people who felt a debt. But he was able to talk Janie around to his old dream of organizing in the South, and she went down there with him.

V

An epitaph for Sidney should explain as well as tell, but how are you to explain what the movement for freedom means for one human being? The papers, the magazines, the press of the whole nation explain why people like Sidney Greenspan are corrupt, evil, selfish, and enemies of mankind, and to that they devote countless millions of words; so, in return, what can one say about Sidney except to state that there was no rest for him so long as one man was enslaved, oppressed, or exploited by another. He went to the South and joined in the struggle to organize the sharecroppers. He spent fourteen months down there, and that was in the area where three organizers were killed—where they simply disappeared, vanished from the face of the earth.

And this he did for thirty dollars a week, to live day in and day out with the threat of the Klan hanging over him, to be shot at three times, to win neither glory nor credit nor wealth nor fame. I remember speaking to him when he was back from that, a few months before he managed to enlist. A group of us were in the little place downtown which he and Janie shared, and someone asked why a person like him did what he did.

"It's not so much," Sidney said. "I saw the party people in Spain. They stayed there. I could go home."

"But why do you do it?"

"Why does any man do anything? The factors in him add up. They make a sum total, and he adds to that out of his understanding. Then he does what he has to do."

Then someone said, "Suppose you won and suppose you built your brave new world, do you think anyone would remember?"

"It isn't important," Sidney answered slowly. "But they'll remember."

Once before, many years ago, when we were very young, and Sidney and a good many more of us were brought into court during the unemployment demonstrations, a magistrate asked him the same question, why he did what he did; and it was then that I realized, for the first time I imagine, with what zest and joy a person can taste of life, for Sidney, leaning forward on the rail, told the magistrate, his voice level:

"You don't question what you do. You do it because you have to—and you're paid for it. You want me to make you understand why I do what I do—could I make you hear a million voices? I'm paid in my own coin!"—holding out an empty hand.

Again, not so long ago, I went to call on the old man Greenspan, still alive, more shriveled, more used up, but still working, and after we had spoken about other things, he asked me:

"Why couldn't Sidney be satisfied to live quiet?"

Seeing the old man with his rheumy eyes, his bent back, his poor swollen feet, I was brought back to the time when I first knew Sidney, and I realized that what he had always wanted was to live quiet, as the old man said, to step into the old, generous stream of life, and to taste it deeply and comfortingly for the time that is given to any man; I had it for a moment, the full answer, and then I lost it.

VI

After Pearl Harbor, Sidney managed to enlist through a fraud. It doesn't hurt to say that. Young as he was, he was no good physically, but he knew an army doctor down at Monmouth, and he got in. But because of the inescapable condition of his eyes, and because of headaches—they called them migraine, but they were the result of fascist efficiency—he was placed in the medics and shipped to a camp in Georgia. For a year and a half he remained in that Georgia camp, and three times he tried to be transferred to the infantry. There were long periods when none of us but Janie heard from him; we went in all directions as the war spread over the face of the earth. I had one letter from him in that time, in which he said:

. . . It's not like Spain. Some officers here found out I was in the Brigade—I never could or wanted to keep my mouth shut—and they gave me no peace, day or night. It's you red bastard this, and you red bastard that, and what did they pay you to go to Spain? I'm trying to get into a combat outfit. In a war, the only safe place, from a mental point of view, is at the front. . . .

He went over to England as a combat medic, and from England into North Africa. In North Africa, he ran into Johnny Graham, from the Brigade, who was with the 1st Rangers. Johnny told me about it afterwards; it was one of those crazy coincidences, which happen so often in life. Johnny fell over with a bad splinter in his thigh, and he was lying in the sand and plucking at it, and plucking at it, and swearing because the amount of blood frightened him and unnerved him, when this small medic crawled up and said, "Let me try," and got the splinter out and put the sulfa on, and was bandaging it when Johnny saw his face and recognized him. That calmed Johnny, and I can understand how he was able to relax, and take the cigarette that was offered to him, and say, "Hullo, Sidney."

"I'm in the medics," Sidney said. "Isn't that a hell of a note. I'm in the medics."

"I'm glad you're in the medics," Johnny said. Just that; then some stretcher-bearers came up, and they took him away. But Johnny afterwards remembered that to be there, Sidney must have come through the Straits, and seen those bare, brown hills that make the southern lip of Spain—because to men like Sidney, there's no end, but always a time when you come back to where you began.

On and off, in the months which followed, someone who knew Sidney would run into him, first in Sicily, and then in Italy; and then, from that and from those who had never known him before, there grew up a legend about him. There had been no legend from the work he did in Spain and in the States, but now in Italy there was emerging a quality of calm and certainty for men who had no certainty, many of whom didn't know where they were going or what they were fighting for, who only knew that in sunny Italy it rained like hell, and when you got over one mountain, there was another behind it, and that the Nazi was not someone who threw away his gun and surrendered after the first round of artillery; and for these men, Sidney Greenspan was something out of another world and another struggle. He had an answer that no one else could give them, and a faith in men compounded from different stuff than the Nash-Kelvinator ads. It would be said, more and more often, and by more people, "I met a guy called Greenspan, a medic who was in Spain—I guess he's a red, but he knows from where—"

One of them, who had looked up Janie when he came back to the States, said, "You'd be afraid, you'd be so goddamn afraid, and then you'd talk to Sidney, and it would be all right."

VII

He was killed at the beginning of '44. The United States Army, considering it above and beyond the call of duty, wrote in its citation:

Private First Class Sidney Greenspan, Medical Department.

Near Carano, Italy, January 24, 1944, he crawled sixty yards under enemy machine gun fire to administer first aid to a wounded infantryman and then continued forward another fifty yards to care for two more wounded infantrymen. He administered first aid to one of the men and dragged him into a covered position. He then returned to the other man and treated him. While so doing his right hip was shattered by machine gun fire and a second burst splintered his left forearm. Nevertheless, and in spite of severe bleeding which he could not quench, he finished administering aid to the wounded man and dragged him to a place of cover. He then crawled 60 yards in an effort to regain contact with his unit, but was forced to discontinue from weakness caused by loss of blood. Death resulted from shock and loss of blood.

I guess the best way to tell such a thing is the way the Army tells it, as a routine job by the T-4 who writes citations as the casualties come in. They are not bothered with reasons or subjective factors, and having a war against fascism to win, they could be more objective about a man like Sidney than certain people who write about such things today. Sidney's name was brought up for the Congressional Medal of Honor, but that was a big-time operation, and they went into his past, and the matter was dropped.

And that could be left out of an epitaph for Sidney. There will be other awards some day, other citations, and when that time comes the stones and the fields and the broken cities will give tongue and speak of all the nameless. They buried Sidney Greenspan in Italian soil, good soil; and the soil of Spain is good, too, and the soil of America, and the soil of the Soviet Union, and of China—and if he had his choice, I don't think there is any place he wouldn't have been at home, fully and completely at home.

Some of us who knew him, when we heard of his death, thought that we would write down an epitaph for him. Then, in the personal columns of the paper he read and loved, there were many boxes with heavy black lines to bind them in, and whatever the name, there was a reference to the struggle against fascism. That was how we came to put together what we knew and remembered of Sidney; but nothing we could tell and nothing we could compile and no reasons we could give were enough to explain the fabric of him. So we gathered it into a word and wrote: "To the memory of Sidney Greenspan, anti-fascist, who fell in the people's struggle—from his comrades."

Where Are Your Guns?

IN THE LAND of the goyim, my father traded with the Indians. We traded for beaver, and my father's word was as good as his bond, and we never carried a weapon except for our knives. From the lakes in the north to the canebrake in the south and as far west as the great river—there we traded and we never carried a weapon, never a musket or a rifle or a pistol, for these are weapons of death; and if you deal with death, what else can you expect in return? Is it not said in the Book, "Thou shalt not hate thy brother in thy heart?" And is it not also said, "I will also give thee for a light to the Gentiles"?

Among the Mingoes, we dwelt and traded and among the Delawares, too, and among the Wyandottes and the Shawnees and the Eries and the Miamis and the Kickapoos, and even among the Menomini, where only the French have been, and never did we carry a weapon. "Men do not kill for the sake of killing," my father answered once to a hunter who could not understand why we didn't walk in fear of the red savage. "My people walked in fear for too long," my father said. "I don't fear what is different."

The hunter was one who slew his meat and ate it, even as the red men do, but our law is different. We kept the Law. Would you understand if I told you how we suffered to keep the Law? The Law says that when a beast is slain, it must be with the hand of a holy man, so that the lifeblood will run out as an offering to God rather than as a wanton slaughter of one of His creatures—with God's will and God's blessing.

Long, long, ago, when I was only nine, my father said, "The high holy days are coming, and we have not sat down with our own people since your mother's death three years ago," speaking in the old tongue, which he taught me so carefully, being a man of learning. "I would have you pray for your mother's soul, and I would be with my own people for a little while, there is such a hunger in me." So we saddled our horses and made the long journey eastward to Philadelphia, where were a handful of our own people. Not that they welcomed us so well, we were two such wild buckskin folk, my father's great black beard falling to his waist; but we prayed with them and we ate meat with them.

You would have thought that we were unclean, they were such fine people there in Philadelphia, and when they talked about certain things, politics and who ruled over whom, indeed we sat as silent as the red men in their own woods. What does a man who trades with the Indians know of politics, my father thought? And what is it to a Jew who rules over a land? A Jew is a Jew, whether it be the old world or this new world, where the forest rolls like the sea. But when they talked of the Law and of holy things, then it was different, for my father was a man of learning and when he lifted the meat to his mouth, he pointed out that this was the first meat he or I had eaten in years—and even after that day in Philadelphia, no unclean meat passed our lips.

I speak of this because I must make you understand my father, the man who traded with the Indians, so you will not judge me too harshly. I am not my father. My father fared forth to a wild land from far-off Poland, and of Poland I know no more than a dream and a legend, nor do I care. With his own hands he buried his wife in the wilderness, and he was mother and father to me, even though he left me with the Indians when I was small, and I lived in their lodges and learned their tongue. I am not like my father. He had a dream, which was to trade with the Indians until there was enough money to buy freedom, peace, security—all those things which, so it goes, only money can buy for a Jew; and because he had that dream, he never knew any comfort and the taste of meat was a strange thing to him. A stream of beaver skins went back to the Company on the donkeys and the flatboats that were owned by the Company, and all of it went to a place called London, and in this place there was a thing called an *account*.

Those were names and words and without meaning to me. I cared nothing of the beaver skins and nothing of the acount, but if my father said that these things were of such importance, then indeed they were, even as the Law was. I knew other things; I knew the talk of the Shawnees and Algonquin talk, and I could make palaver with the men of the Six Nations too, if need be. I knew Yankee talk, the talk of those long-boned hunters of the East, and I knew the French talk and the high-pitched nasal talk of the British, who claimed to own the land, but knew nothing of it and stayed huddled in their outposts and stockades. I spoke the old language of the Book and I knew the Law, and I could catch trout with my bare hands and steal the eggs from under the nesting bird never disturbing it. I knew the step and the stride of nineteen moccasins, and where the wild parsnip grows and the wild turnip too, and with only a knife I could live the year round in the dark woods, where never the sky is seen. By heart in the old Hebrew, I knew the Song of Songs, which is Solomon's, and I knew forty psalms. And from the time I was thirteen, I prayed twice a day.

I also knew what it is to be a Jew.

But not like my father, whom you would have remembered, had you seen him come into Fort Pitt on that day. My father was six feet and two inches tall; fifteen stone he scaled, and never an ounce of fat, but hard as rock, with a black beard that fell to his waist. All through the woods, in those times, were Jews who traded with the Indians and went where no other white man had ever trod, but there was no one like my father, you may believe me. No one so tall or so wide or so heavy—or so sweet of speech and gentle of mien, yet I remember so well a cart and horse mired belly-deep, and my father heaved the horse out and the cart too. Or the time a year before at the company post of Elizabeth, where two Delawares were crazed with drink; they would have been slain, for what is better sport for a redcoat than to slay a drunken Indian? But my father lifted them from the ground like puppies and shook them until the drink went out of them, and instead of going to their deaths they went home to their lodges and were grateful.

I am not like my father, believe me. No man touches my forehead, unless he kill me first; but when a hunter met my father and saw that he was a Jew and begged to feel for the two horns nestling in his hair, my father would smile and agree, and then kindly commiserate with the man when he discovered that the old wives' tale was no more than that. Nor did my father sign for surety—ever, be it old MacTavish, who fended for the company in the north, or Ben Zion, who provided trade goods in Philadelphia, or Pontiac, whom my father told me to look at and heed, so I would know what was best in my own people in the ancient time when they followed the way of war and not of peace.

That was my father, who bound the phylacteries on his

head faithfully every morning, and kept the Law and did justice to all who knew him. That was my father, who came into Fort Pitt with me on this day. We drove seven donkeys and they carried eleven hundred skins, and for a month I had listened to my father plan how now we would go to New York and demand an accounting for the Company, and there we would live with our own people and roam the woods no more. He was filled with it. A mile from the fort, we had stopped to drink water at the outhouse and mill of McIntyre, and my father told him.

"No more this way, Angus," my father said, "but eastward and the boy will wear woven cloth on his back."

"Ye been a woodsy man these twenty year," MacIntyre said somberly.

"I'll be woodsy no more. And young Reuben here will make a company of his own, the good Lord willing."

"Heed the new commandant. He has no love for Jews, or for Scots either. I am glad to see you safe, because there is war with the Mingoes."

My father laughed because we had bought two hundred skins from the Mingoes, and there was no war talk in their cities. But when we came to the fort, there was a new guard at the gate. The doors were closed, and the men on the walls wore yellow facings and shakos I had not seen before. It was a new regiment for the woods.

"Who goes there?" a sergeant called.

"Two traders with skins."

"And where are your guns?"

"We bear no guns," my father said. "We are Jews who trade with the Indians."

Then the doors opened, and we entered with our donkeys, but there was never a smile or a nod. I looked at my father and he looked at me, but there was nothing to make out of his face; and when we looked around us, we saw that these were new men. Their cloth clothes were still fresh with the East, and they stared at us as if we were creatures; were we not Jews, they would have stared at us too, but there was that in their eyes that was singular for Jews.

Where, I wondered, were the Yankee folk, Benson, the smith, Bryan, the cooper, Wheelbury, the harness maker? Where were the Indians, who were always a crowd in the fort? Where were the woodsy folk, the hunters, the French, in their green buckskin and red hats? Where were Stuart and Stevenson, the storekeepers? That too was in my father's mind, as I could see, but his broad face was calm, and he smiled at me as we prodded our donkeys into the low town. As if this were the first time we had come to old Duquesne, soldiers barred our way and a British subaltern demanded of us:

"Who are you and what are your names?"

"We are Jews who trade with the Indians," my father said. "My name is David, and this is my son, Reuben. Twelve years I have been in and out of this place, even when it was Duquesne, and I am known in the forest country."

"I don't know you," the young man said, as if we were dirt and less than dirt.

"Then I be sorry," my father said. "Stevenson knows me, for I have always traded with him and paid my loanings. Benson knows me, for he shod my beasts, and Bryan knows me, for he boxed my goods. I am not a stranger here."

"You are a Jew and damned insolent," the young man replied. "As for the scum of this place, they know the dregs of the woods. Where are your arms?"

"We bear no arms but our knives."

"And how did you come through the Mingoes? There is

war with the Mingoes.''

A mass of soldiers were around us now, and now I could see Benson and some of the others, but keeping off. I am not like my father. I would have made a story then, but it was not in him to speak anything but the truth. He was going to New York, but I knew of a sudden that he would be lonely and forsaken in such a place. The green woods was his home, and it was not in him to speak anything but the truth.

"There is no war with the Mingoes," he said slowly. "I traded two hundred skins with the Mingoes, and I lay in their lodges this fortnight past. There is no war with the Mingoes."

The young officer said, "You're a damned liar, a filthy Jew, and a spy as well."

My father's face was sad and hard and woeful. I moved, but he moved quicker, and he struck the officer a blow that would have felled an ox. Then we fought a little, but there were too many of them.

They put us in a cell and they gave us no food and no water. We were bleeding and bruised, but it was not hard to go without food. It was hard for my father to go without his phylacteries, but after the second day I didn't care. They came every few hours and asked us to tell what we knew of the Mingoes, but what we knew was of no interest to them.

The colonel came finally. It is so different now that you cannot know what a colonel was in those days in a place like Fort Pitt. He was an English gentleman and he was God too, and he prodded us with his stick.

"How old are you?" he asked me.

"I am fifteen," I croaked.

"You are large for fifteen," he lisped, holding a lace handkerchief over his nose. "The Yankees come large, but I should not think it would be so with a Jew. I shall hang your father tomorrow, but if you will tell me what you know of the Mingoes, you may go free and take your seven beasts with the skins.''

''I know nothing of the Mingoes.''

''And how do you travel in the woods without guns? I am very curious.''

''That you could never know,'' my father said, almost sadly.

Even these days you hear things said of Jews; it is that way; but once my father found a robin with a broken wing, and made splints for the wing and a sling, so that we could carry the bird with us, and he nursed it until it flew away. So I will remember until I die how the British drums rolled as they hanged my father, who traded with the Indians in the land of the goyim, and whose word was as good as his bond. And then they gave me thirty lashes until I bled like a pig, and drove me from the fort to die in the forest.

A Jew dies hard, they say. I crawled a mile to Angus Mac-Intyre's mill, and he washed my back and cared for me until I returned to my senses and could walk again.

''Weep for your father,'' he said, ''for you are only a laddie, and he was much of man.''

''I weep no more and pray no more. My father is dead, and I am not like him.''

''You will be like him, lad.''

''I will never be like him, Angus, but I will make my word like my bond. I give you my word I will bring you forty beaver skins if you give me a musket and powder and shot.''

A long time the old Scot looked at me, measuring me and weighing me. ''Go to the land of the Yankees, lad,'' he said, ''and wear woven clothes on your back.''

''The Yankees stood by while my father was hanged. When that redcoat filth drove the Mingoes from the fort, the

Yankees stood by. When two Mingoes came back for the little they left behind and were slain at the gate, the Yankees said nothing."

"How many of them were there?" the Scot said quietly. "They are a strange folk, dirty and bragging and mean and sometimes, in a most curious way, a little noble. Will they be silent forever?"

"Will you give me the gun?"

"You are one of them," the Scot said.

"When they are no longer silent—I will be one of them. When they strike, I will strike with them."

"And your father traded in the woods with never more than a knife. For the Company. Are you for the Company?"

"I am against any man in a uniform."

"I will give you the gun, lad," the Scot said sadly, "and you will slay your meat and eat it."

"And other things."

"Then put no price on it, for what you seek has no price but a man's blood. You are one of them."

He gave me the gun, and I left him and walked eastward.

Spoil the Child

THE FIRST MORNING Pa was gone, I tried to ride one of the mules. I didn't think that would hurt, because the mules were unharnessed anyway. But Maude told Ma, and Ma licked me. Ma was in the wagon, and she wouldn't have seen. I told Maude I'd remember.

Pa left about six in the morning while Ma still slept. "Goin' after meat?" I asked him. He had his rifle.

He nodded.

"Kin I go?"

"Stay with Ma, Sonny," he said. "She ain't well."

"You said I could hunt—"

"You stay with Ma, Sonny."

Maude got up a few minutes after that. I could see Pa like a black dot out on the prairie. I pointed to him.

I said: "That's Pa out there huntin'."

Maude was combing her hair, not paying a lot of attention to me. Then I tried to ride the mule. Pa would never let me ride his horse. It was only half-broken, cost four hundred dollars. Ma was always saying we could have lived a year on what that horse cost.

Maude woke Ma. My mother was a tall, thin women, tired looking. She wasn't well. I could see that she wasn't well.

"Dave, get off that mule," she said. "Where's Pa?"

"Went out to hunt."

"Come here. Can't ever get it into your head to behave."
I went over, and she slapped my face. "Don't bother them
mules. When'll he be back? We can't stay here."

"He didn't say."

"Get some chips for a fire," Ma told me. "My land, I
never seen such a lazy, shiftless boy." But she didn't say it the
way she always did, as if she would want to bite my head off.
She seemed too tired to really care.

I guess Ma licked me every day. She said I was bad—a lot
worse than you'd expect from a boy of twelve. You didn't
expect them to be bad that young.

"You learn to leave the mules alone," Maude called.

"You shut up," I told her. Maude was fifteen, and pretty.
She had light hair, and a thin, delicate face. Ma said that some
day Maude would be a lady. She didn't expect much from me.
She said I would be like Pa.

I walked away from the wagon, looking for chips. By now,
Pa was out of sight, and where he had gone the prairie was just
a roll of yellow and brown, a thread of cloud above it. It frightened me to be alone on the prairie. Pa laughed at it, and called
it a big meadow. But it frightened me.

We had been on the prairie for a week now. Pa said in
another few weeks we'd reach Fort Lee, due west. He said that
if he had cattle stock, he'd settle down right on the prairie.
This way, he'd cross the mountains, grow fruit, maybe, in
California. Ma never believed much he said.

I went back to the wagon and started a fire. Ma had gone
inside, and Maude sat on the driver's seat.

"You might gimme a hand," I told Maude.

"I don't see you overworking," Maude said.

"You better learn to shut up."

From inside the wagon, Ma yelled: "You hold your tongue, David, or I'll wallop you!"

"You're a little beast," Maude said.

"You wait," I told her.

I went to the keg, drew some water, and set it up to boil. I could tell by the sound that there wasn't a lot of water left in the keg. Pa had said we'd reach water soon.

When I came back to the fire, I glanced up at the sky. It was an immense bowl of hot blue, bare except for a single buzzard that turned slowly, like a fish swimming. I guess I forgot. I kept looking up at the buzzard.

Ma climbed down from the wagon slowly. "You're the same as your Pa," she said. "Lazy an' bad." Her face was tight-drawn. For the past few weeks she had hardly smiled, and now it seemed that she wouldn't smile again.

"And fresh," Maude said.

I put the water on the fire, not saying anything.

"Spare the rod and spoil the child," Ma said.

Then her face twisted in pain, and she leaned against the wagon. "Well, don't stand there," she told me. "Water the mules."

I went to the keg. I knew there wasn't enough water for the mules. I hoped Pa would come back soon; I had a funny, awful fear of what would happen if he didn't come back soon. I kept glancing out at the prairie.

Pa had an itch in his feet. Ma said I would grow up the same way—having an itch in my feet. She was always sorry that she had married a man with an itch in his feet. Sometimes she said that the war had done it, that after the war between the North and the South, men were either broken or had to keep moving, like Pa. Always west.

We lived in Columbus. Then we moved to St. Louis; then to Topeka. Pa couldn't stop, and Pa got more and more worn-out. She said that a wild land was no place to raise children. It was hard on Ma, all right. Pa didn't do much, except when we were moving west, and then he would be like a different person. Ma never complained to him. She licked me instead.

I gave the mules enough water to cover the bottoms of their pails.

Ma came over, said: "That's not enough water."

"There ain't a damn sight more."

"Don't swear!" Ma exclaimed. She clapped a hand across my head.

"He's always swearing," Maude said. "Thinks he's grown-up."

Ma stared at me a moment, dully; then she went over and prepared breakfast. It was gruel and hardtack.

"Fresh meat would be good," Ma said. She looked over the prairie, maybe looking for Pa. I knew how much she cared for Pa. She would talk a lot about itching feet, but that didn't matter.

After breakfast, I gave the mules some oats, and Maude cleaned up the dishes. I kept glancing at Maude, and she knew what I meant. She didn't care, until Ma went back into the wagon. It hurt me to look at Ma.

"He'll be back soon, I guess," Ma said. Then she climbed into the wagon. It was a big sixteen-foot wagon, the kind they called freighters, with a hooped top, covered with dirty brown canvas.

Maude said: "You leave me alone."

"I'll leave you alone now," I told Maude. "I gotta leave you alone now. Maybe you know what's the matter with Ma?"

"That's none of your business," Maude said.

"It's my business, all right."

"You're just a kid."

I went to the back of the wagon and pulled out Pa's carbine. It was the one he had used during the war, a short cavalry gun.

Ma saw me; she lay inside, and I could hear her breathing hard. She said: "What're you up to now—Pa back?"

"Not yet."

"Well, you tell me soon as he gets back. And don't get into any mischief."

"All right."

In front of the wagon, I sat down on a feed box, and cleaned the gun with an old rag. Maude watched me. Finally, she said: "I'm gonna tell Ma you're fooling with Pa's gun."

"You keep your mouth shut."

Ma groaned softly then, and we both turned around and looked at the wagon. I felt little shivers crawl up and down my spine. Where was Pa? He should have been back already. I put down the gun and walked around the wagon. In a circle, the prairie rose and fell, like a sea of whispering yellow grass. There was nothing there, no living thing.

Maude was crying. "Why don't Pa come back?" she said.

I didn't answer her. I guess it occurred to me for the first time that Pa might not come back. I felt like crying. I felt like getting into a corner and crying. I hadn't felt so small for a long time. It would be a comfort to have Ma lick me now. You get licked, and you know you're a kid, and you don't have to worry about anything else.

I said to Maude: "Go inside the wagon and stay with Ma."

"Don't you order me around."

"All right," I said. I turned my back on her. I didn't hold much with girls when they're that age.

Then Maude went inside the wagon. I heard her crying, and I heard Ma say: "You stop that crying right now."

I loaded the carbine. I untethered one of the mules, climbed onto it, and set out across the prairie in the direction Pa had taken. I didn't know just what I'd do, but I knew it was time Pa came back.

It wasn't easy, riding the mule just with harness straps. Mules have a funny gait. And we didn't go very fast. I was glad Ma and Maude were in the wagon, otherwise Ma would probably lick the pants off me.

In about a half hour, the wagon was just a tiny black dot. It might have been anything. I kept glancing at the sun to remember the direction I had taken. Then a swell hid the wagon. I kept on going. I knew that if I stopped, even for a little while, I'd cry my head off.

I saw a coyote. He stood like a dog and watched me. An antelope hopped close, and I might have shot at him. But I couldn't bring myself to fire a rifle there. It would have done something to me.

I found Pa. I guess I had been riding for about an hour when I saw him, over to one side. A buzzard flapped up, and I felt my throat tighten until I thought it would choke me. I didn't want to go over to him. I got down from the mule, and I walked over slowly. But I didn't want to; something made me.

He was dead, all right. Maybe it was Indians and maybe it wasn't; I didn't know. He was shot four times, and his gun was gone.

The buzzard wouldn't go away; I shot the buzzard. I didn't cry. The carbine kicked back and made my shoulder ache. I was thinking about how Pa always called me an undersized, freckled little runt. He said I wouldn't grow up. Maybe that's why I didn't cry.

I went away a little distance and sat down. I didn't look at Pa. I tried to remember where we were, what Pa had told me about going west. When I thought of Ma, I had a sense of awful fear. Suppose it happened now.

The mule walked over and nuzzled my shoulder. I was glad the mule was there then. If he wasn't, I don't know what I would have done.

Pa had to be buried. I knew that men had to be buried, but I couldn't do it. The prairie was hard, baked mud. I went back to Pa and stood over him; I guess that was the hardest thing I had ever done in my life. I straightened his clothes. I pulled off his boots. Men in the West were always talking about dying with their boots on. I didn't know how it meant anything, one way or another, but I thought Pa would be pleased if he didn't have his boots on.

Then I climbed up on the mule and started back for the wagon. I tried not to think that I was twelve years old. If you get to thinking about that, they you're no good at all. When I got back, Ma would lick me plenty.

The mule must have found its way back, because I didn't pay much attention to that. I let the reins loose, holding onto the harness straps, and I kept swallowing. Then I saw the wagon.

I thought: "I can't tell Ma now—maybe later." Nobody had ever told me about a thing like that, but I knew it wouldn't do to tell Ma now. I guess I only felt it instinctively, but I knew that the importance wasn't in Pa any more. All that was important was life, and life was just a fleck of dust in the prairie. It was like a nightmare to think of the distance of the prairie, and how we were alone.

I rode up to the wagon, and Maude and Ma were both standing next to it. I could tell from Ma's face how worried she had been about me.

"There he is!" Maude screamed.

Ma said: "I guess there ain't nothing a body can do with you, Dave. Get off that mule."

I slipped off, tethered the mule. My whole body was twisted up with the strain of keeping what I had seen off my face. I came over to Ma.

"Where you been?" she demanded.

"Hunting."

"I reckon there's nothing else for a little loafer like you. Spare the rod and spoil the child. Come here."

I went over and bent down, and she walloped me a bit, not too hard. She wasn't very strong then, I guess. I cried, but I wasn't crying because of the licking. I had had worse lickings than that and never opened my mouth. But it seemed to break the tension inside of me, and I had to cry. I went over and sat down with my back against one of the wagon wheels.

Maude walked past me and said: "I guess that learned you."

I just looked at her, without answering. I took out my jackknife and began to pare at one of the wagon boards. Then my eyes traveled to the water keg.

I got up and went around to Ma. She was still standing there, staring off across the prairie in the direction Pa had gone.

Without turning, she said to me: "Seen anything of your Pa?"

"No."

The sun was westward now, a splotch of red that blazed the whole prairie into a fire. I could get a little of how Ma felt; I could see the loneliness.

"Get a fire going," she said. "He ought to have enough sense to come back early. Stop that whimpering. God help a woman when a man has itching feet."

I gathered chips and started the fire. When I took water from the keg for mush, the keg was just about empty. I didn't mention that to Ma. She went about preparing supper slowly, awkwardly, and Maude watched her, frightened.

Ma kept glancing at the west.

"Be dark soon," I said

"Guess Pa'll be here any minute," Ma said dully. I could tell that she didn't believe that.

"I guess so," I nodded.

We ate without speaking much. Ma didn't eat a great deal. As soon as we had finished, she went into the wagon.

Maude was saying: "I don't see how I can clean dishes without water. You fetch some water, Dave."

"There ain't no water," I said.

Maude stared at me, her eyes wide and frightened. She had heard stories, just the same as I had, about pilgrims who ran out of water. She opened her mouth to say something.

"What about Ma?" I asked her quietly, nodding at the wagon.

"Why don't Pa come back?"

"Ain't no sense thinking about Pa if he ain't here. What about Ma? I guess it won't be long."

She shook her head.

"You don't need to be scared," I muttered. "It won't do no good to be scared. I reckon the worst part of this trip is over."

"Where's Pa?" she whispered. "What happened?"

"How do I know what happened? You girls make me sick. I never seen anything to beat you girls."

I got up and went over to the water keg. I shook it, hoping, without having any reason to hope. I knew it was just about empty. We had plenty of food—dried meat and meal and dried beans—enough to last a month, I guess. But Ma would need water.

Maude was crying.

"Why don't you go to bed?" I said. "Go in and sleep with Ma. I'll stay out here."

"You're not big enough to stay out here alone," Maude said, but I knew she was afraid to stay inside the wagon with Ma. I knew how she felt, and I didn't blame her for the way she felt, she was such a kid, with Ma petting her all the time. We couldn't talk it over between ourselves, and that would have made it a lot better. But we couldn't.

"I'm plenty big enough," I said.

Inside the wagon Ma groaned, and out on the prairie a coyote was barking. There's nothing like a coyote barking to make your insides crawl. I was all shivers, and I could see that Maude wanted to stay close to me. But that wouldn't have made it any better.

"Get in the wagon, damn you!" I cried. I was glad Ma couldn't hear me swear. Ma would lick me good and plenty when I swore like that.

Surprised, Maude stared at me. Then, without a word, she went into the wagon.

I stood there, outside, for a while. It had grown quite dark. In the sky there was a faint reflected light of the sun, but it was quite dark. I walked over to the wagon and picked up one of the mule blankets. It was a warm night, summertime; I decided to put the blanket under the wagon and lie down on it.

I heard Maude saying her prayers in the wagon, but no sound from Ma. I couldn't say my prayers. Usually, Ma saw to it that I did, but tonight I couldn't say a word aloud. I tried, opening my mouth, but no words came out. I thought them, as much as I could. I tried not to think about Pa. Spreading the blanket, I lay down on it, holding the carbine close to me.

It seemed a part of Pa and all that was left; I hugged it.

I couldn't sleep. I tried for a long time, but I couldn't sleep. It was quite dark now, with no moon in the sky. The mules were moving restlessly; probably because they wanted water.

I think I dozed a little. When I opened my eyes again, the moon was just coming up, yellow and bloated. I felt chilled thoroughly. Bit by bit, what had happened during the day came back, and now it was all more real than it had been in the daytime. While I lay there, thinking about it, I heard horses' hoofs; at first not noticing them, and only becoming aware of them when the horses bulked out of the night, two men riding slowly.

They were in the moonlight, and I was hidden in the shadow of the wagon. They didn't see me. They stopped just about a dozen yards from the wagon, sitting on their horses and eyeing the mules. The mules moved restlessly.

When I realized they were Indians I couldn't move, just lay there and watched them. They were naked to the waist, with their hair in two stiff braids to their shoulders. They both carried rifles.

I thought of Pa. I thought of screaming to wake Maude and Ma. I thought: "If they shot Pa—"

They were cutting loose the mules.

I felt for the carbine, twisted around, so I lay on my belly. One of the men had dismounted and was coming toward the wagon. He held his gun in one hand and had drawn a knife with the other. I sighted the center of his breast and fired.

I remember how the sound blasted out the silence of the prairie. In the wagon, someone screamed. The Indian stopped, seemed to stare at me, swayed a bit, and crumpled to the ground. I remember the sharp pain in my shoulder from the blow of the recoil.

The mounted man's horse had wheeled about. He pulled it back, and fired at me. The shot threw sand in my face. I had a few cartridges and caps in my pocket, and I tried frantically to reload. The cartridges slipped through my fingers.

Then the Indian was gone. He had taken the other horse with him, and I heard their hoofs thundering across the prairie. I dropped the carbine. My shoulder ached terribly. Inside the wagon, Maude was whimpering, my mother groaning.

I climbed from under the wagon. The Indian lay on his back, his face hard and twisted. I stood there, looking at him.

Maude climbed down out of the wagon. "What is it?" she cried. Then she saw the Indian and screamed.

"All right—I shot him."

She stood there, holding her hand to her mouth.

"You get back in the wagon. I guess he killed Pa, all right. Don't tell that to Ma."

She shook her head. Ma was groaning. "I can't go back," Maude said.

"Why?"

And then I knew. I should have known from the way Ma was groaning. I went up to Maude and slapped her face. She didn't seem to feel it. I slapped her again.

"Get in there!" I yelled.

We had lanterns on the outside of the wagon. I took one and lit it. I wasn't trembling so much now. I gave the lantern to Maude, who was still standing the way she had been before.

"Go inside," I said.

Maude climbed into the wagon, taking the lantern with her. Then I cried. I crouched under the wagon, clutching the carbine and crying.

Finally, I went over to the Indian. I forced myself to do that. He lay half across the rifle he had carried. I pulled it out, and it was my father's rifle, all right.

I don't know how long I stood there holding the rifle. Then I put it under the seat, along with the carbine. I didn't want to look at the wagon.

I walked over to the mules. It was hard to harness them. When it was done, I ached all over, and my shoulder was swollen where the carbine had rested.

I climbed to the driver's seat. The curtains were down, and I couldn't see into the wagon, but the light still burned. Taking down Pa's whip, I let it go onto the mule's backs. I had seen Pa do that and sometimes he let me try. The whip was fourteen feet long and I couldn't do much with it, but I got the mules moving. They had to keep moving. We had to find water.

At night, under the moon, the prairie was black and silver at the same time. Somehow, it didn't frighten me the way it had during the day. I sat there thinking, I guess, of nothing at all, only awfully aware of the change inside me.

We drove on like that. I kept the mules at a slow pace, so the freighter wouldn't roll much. I was very tired, and after a while I didn't use the whip at all.

Then Maude came out of the wagon, sat down next to me. She looked at me and I looked at her, but she didn't say anything. She pressed close to me.

I whistled at the mules.

Inside the wagon something was whimpering. It made me tremble to hear that.

"Reckon we'll find water soon" I told Maude.

She nodded mechanically. Her head kept nodding and I dozed, myself. I guess I kept dozing through the night, fell asleep toward morning.

Maude woke me. The wagon had stopped, and the sun was an hour up. The mules had stopped on the bank of a slow, brown stream, lined with cottonwoods as far as I could see.

Maude was pointing at the water.

"Don't you start crying now," I said, rubbing my eyes.

"I won't," Maude nodded.

Ma called me, not very loud: "Dave, come here."

I climbed inside the wagon. Ma was lying on the bed, her arm curled around something. I peered at it.

"Do you know?" she said.

"I reckon I do. I reckon it's a boy. Girls ain't much use."

Ma was crying—not much; her eyes were just wetting themselves slowly.

"Where are we?" Ma asked me.

"We been traveling through the night. There's a river out there. I guess we don't need to worry about water."

"All night—Pa back?"

I said slowly: "I killed an Indian last night, Ma. He had Pa's gun."

Then she just stared at me, and I stood there, shifting from one foot to another, wanting to run away. But I stood there. It must have been about five minutes, and she didn't say anything at all. The baby was whimpering.

Then she said: "You harnessed the mules?"

"Uh-huh. Maude didn't help me—"

Ma said: "You don't tease Maude. You don't tease Maude, or I'll take a stick to you. I never seen a boy like you for teasing."

"Uh-huh," I nodded.

"Just like your Pa," Ma whispered. "It don't pay to have a man whose heels are always itching—it don't pay."

"No use cryin'," I said.

Ma said: "What are we going to do?"

"Go on west. Ain't hard now to go a few hundred miles more. Reckon it won't be hard. Pa said—"

Ma was staring at me, her mouth trembling. I hadn't ever seen her look just like that before. I wanted to put my head down on her breast, hide it there.

I couldn't do that. I said: "Pa told me. We'll go west."

Then I went outside. I sat down on the wagon seat, looking at the river. I heard the baby making noises.

I said to Maude: "A man feels funny—with a kid."

The Little Folk from the Hills

THIS THING HAPPENED to me in an old, old land, where I had
been riding forever with a tech sergeant, a staff sergeant and
two thousand pounds of United States mail. The train stopped
every six miles or so, and each time there was no real certainty
that it would ever start again. We were at Agra or Lucknow or
Patna or some place like that; it doesn't matter very much, and
one town looks like another in such a land. When we rolled
into a town to stay for an hour or six hours or maybe all night,
a bearer in a green and red and white uniform, with a great
piled white turban topped by a splendid feather, more impos-
ing than a Coldstream Guard on dress parade, leaped onto
the running board outside of our compartment and said, "Tea,
sahib?" or "Tray, sahib?"

Whether he said tea or tray depended upon what arrangements we had made with the same kind of person ten or fifty
miles back. The time of day had nothing to do with it. In that
sun-kissed land which the British had civilized, it was always
teatime, in the middle of the night and at dawn, too, and if
the man with the turban said, "Tea, sahib?" he had the tray
on his hand; a juggler, acrobat and waiter rolled up together
but he never missed, and he always knew if there was a dirty
empty tray in the compartment.

We talked a lot about it, about this amazing piece of organization in an essentially unorganized land. In the compartment behind us, two English officers were riding, and I even talked to them about it. One was a subaltern, as they say, and the other was a colonel.

"Never thought about it," the colonel said. "I don't see why you chaps should be so disturbed."

"It's like a game," I explained. "When you got nothing else to talk about."

"You might ask the station commissioner next place we stop."

"That's too easy. Then we got nothing to talk about."

The two Englishmen were very nice and very pleasant. Every now and then I'd spend a couple of hours in their compartment. They had a few bottles of Scotch and gin, and they made you feel that nothing made them happier than for you to be drinking their liquor. But they didn't understand our ways or our methods of thought. The older one, for instance, the colonel, had been in India for thirty years, but it never occurred to him to question how, over a system of maybe a thousand towns and villages, they kept track of those tea trays. It impressed us as organization, perhaps the best piece of organization in the entire theater, but they weren't impressed that way by organization.

The tech sergeant and the staff sergeant didn't like the Englishmen and weren't convinced by what I said about their being nice.

"Limeys are nice," the staff sergeant admitted. "They crap on you with niceness."

"Everything nice," the tech sergeant said. "They live nice. They fight a war nice. They cut your throat nice."

"If they're so damned nice, why don't you ask them if this

rattler has a schedule?''

"They say shedule," the tech sergeant said.

"I asked them. They think maybe it had a schedule, but not in wartime."

"Like the train from Laredo to Mexico City—you add thirty-two hours to the schedule and then chop it up. But you got to be an Einstein to figure it out."

"Did you ask them about the bloody tea trays?"

"They don't know. They suggested I ask the station commissioner next place we stop."

"Isn't that just like a Limey?" the staff sergeant asked.

"Well, they seem interested now. That's the way they are —it takes a little time for them to get interested in something. I'm going to have tea with them and we're going to talk about it some more."

I had tea with them and was in their compartment when we pulled into the station where it happened. I really liked them because they talked so pleasantly about small things. When they asked you a question they didn't really expect any sort of a serious answer; they knew how to talk about things and make conversation. The colonel said he liked Bengal because the hunting was good, but when he learned that I didn't hunt or care anything about it, he sort of apologized. They never said anything that could hurt your feelings. But in a way it put you at a disadvantage.

If you said that the folk were poor, they agreed. "Bloody poor," and with sympathy, speaking of the people with respect and consideration, not as GI's would have spoken about them. The subaltern, who was twenty or twenty-two, had a blond mustache and pink cheeks, and a gentle sweetness that was never disturbed by anything around him. Not by the filth, the misery, the hunger, the heat, the bodies of famine victims along the right of way being eaten by vultures as we watched; not even in Lucknow, where they had three or four hundred dead British soldiers laid out under an awning, plague victims— such a sweetness was all over him, a part of him, that he was nice to the two sergeants, even though they were enlisted personnel. The tech sergeant, commenting on that, said he was a swish.

"A what?" I had asked.

"A swish—a loop."

"A queen, he means," the staff sergeant said. "A rosebud, a pansy."

"He's a gentleman, that's all."

"And who says a loop can't have nice manners?"

But he wasn't that, I said to myself on this day, just a nice young fellow. We were slowing down from what was our usual lightninglike sixteen miles an hour to come into a station, and the subaltern thought it was Crumar, but said so apologetically with a deprecating smile.

"I try to memorize the stations."

"Too many of them," the colonel said.

I thought that someone must know them, the conductor or somebody. "Or timetables," I said.

"A bloody waste of time," the colonel thought.

And anyway, the stations are all the same. In the north there are deserts and in the south there are rice fields, but always a wooden platform with the three tanks of water, one for Hindu soldiers, one for Moslem soldiers and one for British soldiers. Always the food vendors, when there is food, the water vendors, the soft-drink vendors. Always the crowds, the endless stream of people going somewhere or coming from somewhere. Wrapped in white, clean white and dirty white, men in white and women in white, they mill around the stations. They come early; they bring their food; the smell of curry fills the air, and they wait and wait. When the train comes in, they make a rush for it, stuff themselves into the compartments, hang onto the running board. They did it this time, but with a new element, for there were a hundred or so little people, dark and naked, carrying spears and little leather shields, and bows and arrows, too, making a great rush for the train, but a rush that had in it a tired note of hopelessness that you saw at the first glance.

"I'll be damned," the colonel said.

The subaltern smiled gently as the train guards interposed themselves and firmly pushed the little people back.

"Woollies," the colonel said. "And where do you suppose they come from?" He was more moved than the subaltern, who merely remarked, "You would think they'd put some clothes onto them."

"Why?" I asked.

"You know—decent, and all that."

The train guards were neither cruel nor hard; they were simply firm. They pushed the little people away, and the little folk had not much heart in it and gave it up rather easily.

I got out of the compartment and went back to the mail. "In this country," the tech sergeant said, "anything can happen. Jesus God, anything can happen. It could rain balls."

"What do the Limeys say?" the staff sergeant asked.

"They say they shouldn't be undressed."

"So they hocked their clothes. I'm going over to look." We locked up the mail, and the three of us went over together.

"What about the train?" asked the tech sergeant. "How long does she sit here?"

We guessed one and two and three hours, but in any case this was not something you could pass by without seeing.

Alongside the station there was a broad field of sun-baked clay and a little parched grass. It was out in the center of this field that the little people had made their encampment and built small stick fires and raised a few hide lean-tos. There they were, a hundred or a hundred and fifty of them, a whole people, a tribe, a village, a folk, as some would say, with their old and their young, their graybeards, their infants and their children.

They were small people; none of the men were more than five feet in height; the women were like large dolls and the children were like small, fragile dolls. The men and women were tired and hopeless looking, but the tiny children were like other children, even laughing just a little. In color they were a deep yellow-brown, and their eyes made you think of Chinese, but they were not Chinese and they were not anything else that had ever been itemized, catalogued or studied. They wore no clothes, except for a shred of G-string on the men and sometimes a bit of leather on the women, yet they had no consciousness or knowledge of nakedness; you could see that. Also, the Stone Age was ahead of them. Their spears were sticks of wood with fire-hardened tips. Their bows were toy bows, and their arrows had neither tips nor feathers. Their shields were pieces of dry, untanned hide, and their cooking pots were molded crudely from clay. They had no footgear whatsoever, but walked barefoot, and there was just a trace of hair on the faces of the men.

I had never seen such people before. Neither had the staff sergeant; neither had the tech sergeant. They were out of the dawn of man; with each other they were gentle and loving and caressing; they fondled each other, they put their arms around each other, they comforted each other. And they were very hungry; their pots were empty, and they were terribly, terribly hungry. Their bones stood out and their flesh had dried away. Even in that hungry land, they were more hungry than just the hungry, and soon they would die because of the hunger.

We walked among them and their large, soft brown eyes followed us. We stopped by a woman with bare, flat, dry breasts, and the tech sergeant pointed to the baby she held in her arms and said, "Jesus God, that kid has been dead a long time. That kid has been dead so long it stinks."

"Who are they?" I wanted to know. "What are they? And where are they from?"

"You stink after four hours in this heat," the staff sergeant said.

"Now I've seen everything."

"Sure you've seen everything. Wherever you are, you see everything. You got a broad Arkansas perspective. The first time you seen a necktie, you seen everything."

The tech sergeant went back to the train and got some rations and some candy we had there. We opened the cans and took the paper off the chocolate, but at first the people wouldn't eat. We had to persuade them to eat, and then they gave it to the children, and the men and women wept and chattered in their strange tongue while the children ate. We spoke to some bearers, some station people, and some of the people who were standing around, but no one knew who they were, or what they were, or where they were from.

Then the train whistle blew, which meant that sometime in the neighborhood of five minutes or an hour the train would start. We walked back, and when we got to our compartment, there in front of it were the two British officers talking to a civilian; and the colonel said to me, "Rum lot, aren't they?"

"Who?"

"The woollies."

"Why do you call them woollies?"

"Got to call them something, don't you know," the pink-cheeked subaltern smiled. "No one really knows who they are or what they are. Can't talk their language and they can't talk ours. Damned shame. They're from up in the hills somewhere and they must have had a hard time of it with famine and all that, and I suppose a rumor reached them about a train being something which takes you from one place where there's no food to another place where there is food, so here they are." He added as an an afterthought, "They've been trying to board every train for six days now."

The civilian's name was Johnson, and he was the local commissioner or something. The colonel introduced him to me, but not to the two sergeants.

"What are you going to do?" I asked.

"What can one do?" Johnson said. "They can't ride the train without tickets, and if they could, where would they ride to? Food is tight. They're not properly the concern of my district in any case."

Then he walked off with the colonel, toward their compartment in the car behind ours. The subaltern lingered. Embarrassed and apologetic, he said something to the effect of their not lasting very long. "Bloody shame and all that, but they are on their last legs. It solves a problem for the poor beggars."

"What do you mean?" the tech sergeant asked.

"He means, you horse's ass, that they'll starve to death in a few days," the staff sergeant said quietly; and then, just as quietly, but deliberately, he said to the subaltern, "You, my friend, are a dirty second-rate son of a bitch—an upstanding pile of crap, if you follow me."

They boy's pink flushed to red; he stiffened, he stared

at the two enlisted men, muttered something. ''Oh, I say,''
or something of that sort, stared at them a moment or two
longer, then turned on his heel and walked away. The train
began to move, and we ran for our compartment. The tech
sergeant seated himself sadly on a mail sack and started to
whistle ''Don't Fence Me In.'' The staff sergeant went to the
toilet bowl where he kept a cake of ice and a few cans of tomato
juice, and proceeded to open one of the cans.

''What in hell did you do that for?'' I asked him finally.

''No more tea? No more nice people to talk to?''

''You hate, but you never hate with your brains. That
was just a nice dumb kid.''

''You want some tomato juice?''

''Sure. I'll pretend it's a Martini.''

''What are you so pissed-off about?'' the tech sergeant
asked me.

''Nothing—nothing, but what a righteous, clean-limbed
race of people we are. Oh, my God, how righteous!''

''To hell with him,'' said the staff sergeant. ''He's got no
more nice people to talk to.''

Who Is He?

MY GOODNESS, YOU would think that Jesus Christ was worse than Al Capone; a name that should not be spoken. I came home and said, "Mamma, who's Jesus Christ?"

She was washing clothes and she kept on washing clothes.

I said, "Mamma, who was he?"

She wrung out a sheet like a big fat sausage. The whole kitchen was full of the good creamy smell of hot, clean clothes. Suds ran from her arms as she wiped her hands on her apron. Her broad face turned to me with an unspoken question; did I want bread and butter and jam or cake and milk?

"I ain't hungry," I said. "Who is Jesus Christ?"

"If you ain't hungry, go and play."

I turned to the window and indicated the pack. They had driven me tight and close, and here I was and there they were. They hung over the fence, and their words were in their motions because all the windows were closed. There were eight of them, and beyond them, down the hill, stretched the ragged fringe of Linday, the curl of the river, the smoking stacks of the factories beyond.

"I got to wait," I said calmly.

"What did you do to them?" she demanded fiercely. "What do they want from you? I'll take my ironing board and break it over their heads! I'll break every bone in their bodies!''

I waited for her rage to pass. "You couldn't catch them," I said.

"Then stay in the house!" She turned back to her washing.

"I killed Christ," I said, pressing my face against the window and showing them that my facial gestures could be as competent as theirs.

"What!"

"That's what I told them."

This time she dried her hands more slowly. She looked at me keenly and curiously and wanted to know "Why did you tell them that?"

"They say I killed him. My God, they don't stop saying I killed him. They threw me into the river because I killed him. When they took off my pants and burned them up, it was because I killed Christ. And I don't even know who he is. So today I said, 'God damn you, I killed him and I'm damn glad.' ''

"Don't use such words," she whispered.

"What words?"

"Damn."

"All right, but that's what I told them."

"You shouldn't have told them that," she said sadly. "When they hit you, come into the house. But don't tell them such things." Then she turned back to her washing.

I knew that it was no use by now, but I kept insisting. "Who was Jesus Christ?" I pestered her. "Who was Jesus Christ?"

"Go read a book."

"Who was Jesus Christ?"

"Leave me alone. Go play."

So that was that. And when I asked my father that night, do you think I got any more satisfaction? Like fun I did.

My father peddled down the valley to Aberlee with a Ford truck. The Ford was a nineteen twenty-seven Model T, and he would say that he pushed it as much as it pushed him. All the way down the river it was corn and cucumber country. He sold to the farmers, and he said it was as hard to sell to farmers as it was to find a good man. When he came home at night, the tiredness stood out all over him. He wasn't a good man to ask questions.

I asked him while he was eating, and he stopped eating and looked at me as if he had never seen me before.

"Who?" he demanded.

"Jesus Christ."

At first he looked mad, so mad that I could feel the rage crackling all over him like electricity; and I was terrified and sorry that I had asked him the question, and would have liked to take it all and cram it back down my throat. But then the anger drained away, and I saw the love come back into his eyes, the same love that was always there when he regarded me, his one child, his son and first-born.

"Ah, ah, ah," he smiled. "And I was going to bite off your nose for a foolish question."

Then he turned back to his meal.

"All day long," Mamma said, "he bothered me with that."

"Enough. For the last time, enough!" Then he pointed a finger at me and said, "That name is something not to mention in this house—never again. For us, such a man does not live."

"Why?"

"Don't ask me why," he said.

I saw how things went, and closed my mouth. That's the best way when you see how things are going.

The next day, I asked Mike Finnegan, the garbage man, all the time cocking an eye over my shoulder for my mother. Mike Finnegan had on his left arm a naked lady, tatooed in pink and yellow, but with a snake covering the part I wanted to see most. Whenever I asked him, he wiggled his muscle and made the lady dance.

I said to him, "Mike, who was Jesus Christ?"

"Holy Christ," he whispered, putting down the can of garbage. "Can it be that in this Christian country a boy of your age don't know the Lord's name?"

"Nobody told me."

"I'm not blaming you," Mike said. "It's others I'm blaming."

"What others?"

"Them that keep you in your heathen ignorance."

"Yes," I nodded.

"And when you mention the name of our Lord," Mike said, "do this." He crossed himself.

"Like this?"

Mike grinned and took away the garbage. I went into the kitchen and said, "Mamma, look," and I crossed myself.

The stinging slap of her hand sent me reeling back against the wall. I began to cry, and then she knelt down next to me and begged my forgiveness.

"I didn't do nothing," I said.

She smoothed my tears away and spoke to me softly and entreatingly. "Look, my little one," she said. "My precious one, listen to me. You got to know how we are and what we are. I can't make you understand because you're just a little boy. But try to see this. A great big ocean of water and in the middle of it one little island of sand. All day and all night for all the years, the ocean tries to wash away the little island of sand. But each grain of sand clings to the next grain. They hold on to each other like when I hold on to you, so tight. And no matter what the ocean tells them, they hold on, and because of that, they're able to look up and see the sun. No matter what black days come, they can still see the shining promise of almighty God. Do you understand, my little one?''

"No," I said.

She smiled and shrugged and said, "Go and play."

"No," I said, and she looked at me and seemed to understand why. She shrugged her shoulders and kissed me.

"Let them say it," she said softly. "They themselves killed him, a long time ago, maybe two thousand years ago. They hated us before that, but when they killed him, they had more reasons to hate us."

"Why?" I demanded.

"Who knows why?" She made faces at me, trying to make me laugh. "Have some bread and butter and milk and play in the house."

"All right," I said.

And I didn't ask that question of anybody else for a long time. But years later, there was a learned man traveling west from Chicago, and he stopped off at our town and stayed at our house because it was the only house of our faith in the town. After dinner, he sat at the table and talked with my parents and I put my chin on my hands and watched him. They talked about this and that and everything.

Finally, the learned man turned to me and said, "It is good for a boy to listen, but even better for a boy to ask certain questions that may be in his mind."

I questioned my father with my eyes, and when he nodded, blurted out, "Who was Jesus Christ?"

Well, what did they expect? Hadn't I waited long enough

with that question gnawing my insides like a rat?

In the deep, ominous silence that followed, I saw the stranger smiling. He answered calmly, the way he had answered twenty other questions during the evening.

"Jesus was a part of the truth."

"What truth?"

"I must apologize," my father began.

"No, no, I am glad he asked that. Who is to say what man the child is father of? Perhaps he too will be part of the same truth."

My father knit his brows. He was an uneducated peddler. I could see that he was determined to listen to the stranger without revealing his own unlearnedness.

"They killed him," I said.

"Because he told them the truth and they feared him. In the same way that they fear every wise man and every good man."

"Why?"

"Because they are afraid of the truth. Because as soon as the truth wins, there will be no more hate. Do you understand?"

I was afraid to say no. I felt small and unworthy.

Almost humbly, my father said, "Go up to bed. It's late."

"Good night," I told them. I was full of fear as I groped my way through the dark up to my room.

The Suckling Pig

HE CALLED MARCUS and said, "I just heard about it. Jack Brady passed away this morning."

"No!"

"Got up, took a shower, began to dress, and then keeled right over."

"No! Heart?"

"That's right. I makes you stop to think. We're none of us as young as we used to be."

"That's the God's honest truth. But a guy like Brady, you'd think he had twenty good years ahead of him."

"Never had a sick day in his life. It makes you stop to think."

"That's the truth. How's his wife taking it?"

"She's making a big thing. But I got my own ideas on that subject."

"I got mine," Marcus said. "I guess I'll see you at the wake."

"I guess so."

After he called one or two more of the boys, he told his girl to get Rialto Liquor to send a case up to Brady's, half Scotch and half bourbon, and to have a big wreath made up out of red and yellow roses.

"I wouldn't think red and yellow roses for a wreath," the girl said.

"What in hell's the difference? Jack Brady liked red and yellow roses."

The rest of the afternoon dragged slowly, interrupted only by phone calls to tell him what he already knew, that Jack Brady had passed away. Thoughts of death, more and more frequent lately, clouded his mind, and he half regretted that he was not a Catholic, like Brady, so he could let others do the worrying for him. At five, he cancelled the tickets for that evening, and went over to Toots's for a drink.

A half a dozen of the boys were there at the bar, and he killed four Scotches with them, and then felt better. They were all men in their middle fifties, about the same age Jack Brady had been, and they thought of themselves as well as Brady.

"Anyway, it's a nice, clean exit," someone said.

"Clean or not, it ain't nice."

"I had dinner with Jack at the Hickory House last night. He didn't have a thing on his mind, except he thought he'd go down to Florida a little early."

"That's the way it is."

"How is Sue taking it?"

"Breaking her heart."

Some of them grinned, and someone said. "It's a goddamned dirty shame, because there never was a finer guy than Jack Brady."

"You can say that again."

It was after seven before they sat down to eat and almost nine before they had finished. He had clams, roast beef, and finished up with a piece of blueberry pie and coffee. He felt full and comfortable and resentful against the wake, and chastised himself with the thought of how it must have seemed to

Brady, just keeling over at the last minute, the way he did.

They ordered a round of brandy, and over it one asked, "Did anyone call the Mayor?"

"Frankie did. Frankie's taking care of the arrangements."

"He would. What about a drink up there?"

Glad he had remembered, he told about the Scotch and bourbon he had ordered— "Not that Jack didn't always have a little on hand."

On their way out, they picked up two sports writers from the *Journal* and Gibbon, from the *Telly*.

"I wrote the obit myself," Gibbon said. "Did you know he was with the old 77th?"

Some did and some didn't.

"He was worth five punks from this fracas. That was a war."

They got into three cabs and rode over to the Park Avenue address. The Garden crowd were just entering the building when they arrived, and everybody paused in front to exchange hellos and introductions in a subdued tone of voice. Then Dan Raye arrived and said that he had cancelled his performance for tonight. They crowded into the elevator.

He felt a little funny about all the big wheels, and began to wonder if he had ever been really close to a big-time operator like Jack Brady. He had thought of the liquor and he had thought of the wreath and he had rushed over before noon to see what he could do, but Brady moved in the top crowd, and it made him question whether he wasn't walking into Brady's death the same way he had walked into his life.

"The hell with it," he told himself. "I had some damn good times with Jack Brady."

Toots had made up a big basket of food, which Joe Schree was carrying, and he wondered now why he had not thought of that himself. But when they got upstairs, there already was a table loaded down with sandwiches, plates of cold cuts, and a suckling pig, half-carved, looking like a monster embryo. At least thirty people had already arrived, and the bar was set up in one corner, with everybody making his own drinks. Helen Canyon was acting as hostess and when he had a moment, he drew her aside and asked about the body.

"It's in the funeral parlor," she said. "It's no use making it worse for Sue than it is."

"Sure," he said, thinking that after all it would be easier for everyone present without Brady also being present. "How is Sue?"

"She's a soldier, all right. She's in the bedroom."

Almost all of the few women there were in the bedroom with Sue. He went in and said a few words to her, and in spite of himself he couldn't help but imagine himself crawling in with her. She was a big, handsome blond with a good figure, and he said to himself:

"What a lousy, cheap line of thought for Brady's wake!"

He went back to the living room and passed an hour or so just milling around and saying hello to various people and being introduced to others as a good old friend of Jack Brady's. It was after ten o'clock now, and some of the people were leaving. He and four or five of the others, all boys who had been pretty close to Jack Brady, stood in the pantry and swapped memories about one thing and another that they had shared with the dead man. A lot of the stories concerned the time Brady was in Chicago, and he felt somewhat left out of them, but when the stories shifted to the close past, he felt more at home, and he told about how he and Brady had shacked up with the Deleharty sisters in Philadelphia.

It was almost eleven when Father Costello came in. Most

of the men still left were pretty drunk by then, but if Father
Costello noticed it, he didn't remark on it. Father Costello was
an old friend of his, and that made him feel better, especially
the way Father Costello sat down next to him and said:

"Well, man comes and man goes, even the best."

"Even the best, Father."

"And somewhere in it there's reason and justice and a
supreme guiding intelligence. That's what's important to
remember."

"I try to remember that, Father. I sure as hell do."

At a quarter to twelve, he called Alice, who should have
just been finishing with a hot glass of milk at home, after the
show, but no one answered the phone, and he said "The
bitch!" sourly, the drinks wearing onto the bottom of his
stomach by now.

A kind of sallow joylessness had settled over the apartment
by one-thirty in the morning, and some of the boys agreed
with him that it did no one any good, least of all Jack Brady,
to spend the night here. Sue had gone to bed and Father Costello had gone home, so they made a few calls and arranged to
go over to the Cub Room. He tried Alice again and told her to
meet him there.

"You sound lit," she said.

"I had a couple of drinks. Jack Brady was maybe the best
friend I had in the world."

They went downstairs and got cabs and went over to the
Stork Club. He felt sick and low and suddenly hungry, and he
kept remembering the roast suckling pig and wishing he had
made a sandwich of it. He asked Alice if she liked roast suckling
pig.

"What a question!"

"Well do you or don't you?"

"I don't. It tastes like baby would taste roasted."

"How in hell do you know what baby would taste like?"

"That's what it would taste like," Alice said stubbornly.

"I ought to kick her in the teeth, the big blond bitch," he said to himself.

"Why don't you order some caviar and toast?" she asked him.

"Because I don't want caviar and toast. Let's go over to Reuben's and have a steak."

"If you want a steak," she said.

But when they got to Reuben's he changed his mind and had scrambled eggs and Nova Scotia salmon. It was four o'clock in the morning when they had finished, and only Ed Hartly of the boys was left. They dropped him off at his place and rode over to her apartment.

He sat down in the bedroom, and as she began to undress he thought to himself, "If she's got one of those wire brassieres on, I'm going to spit right in her face." She had a wire brassiere on. He got up and started out of the room.

"What is it now?" she demanded.

"Nothing. Nothing. I'm going home."

"What did I do now?"

"Nothing. You don't expect me to come out of Jack Brady's wake and crawl into bed?"

"Why not?"

"The hell with you," he said, slamming the door into the face of what she said, something about a suckling pig. As he waited for the elevator, he tried to remember Father Costello's words about reason, justice and something else.

The Rickshaw

IT WAS ONE hundred twenty degrees in the shade but I walked back to the Press Club because I had principles, and one of them was that I would not be drawn by a man who serves the function of a beast. I had lately come from the North, where sometimes it was one hundred forty degrees in the shade, but it was dry there, and in an hour you could dehydrate yourself completely, yet never get a drop of moisture on your shirt. It was not dry here; it was wet, and I got wet, underwear, shirt, pants and all. So I plodded along most uncomfortably, only stopping once in a while beside the ghats, to watch the carefree natives swimming and diving. It looked cool and inviting, but I tempered my envy with the superior knowledge that these were the most carefully sponsored disease-breeders on earth. It was good to be a white man, wise and knowledgeable—an American among white men, which is even better—and to be able to shower and shave and put on clean clothes and order a Tom Collins and sit under an electric fan while I sipped the drink.

There, at a quarter to five, and feeling comfortably cool, I was started on the second one when the sergeant came along and sat down next to me and asked me what I was doing that night.

"Right here," I said. "I intend to have one more drink before dinner, and then I will have my dinner, and then I will return here and have enough drinks to become pleasantly drunk, and then I will go to bed."

"It's a tough war, Mr. Eldridge," the sergeant said.

"For some it is," I agreed. I liked the sergeant, but he was bound to educate me. He was in Signal Service, and getting over something in the general hospital across the road. Now he was at the end of the cure and able to get out each evening, and he liked the food in the Press Club better than what they gave him at the hospital.

"I thought you would like to go to a meeting tonight," he said apologetically, "because there are some people here who would like to see you and talk to you, because you're an American writer, I mean. I mean, there are some trade-union people and some writers, and they would like to talk to you."

"That's fine," I said. "That's fine."

"I mean you don't have to go if you don't want to go, but I told them I thought you would."

"You told them that?"

"Well, I've been eating on you, so I thought something like this—"

"Look, I walked four miles to get back here, and then I took a shower, and now I feel comfortable and cool for the first time today."

"Why didn't you take a rickshaw?"

I explained carefully and slowly that I did not like to be drawn by a man as by a beast. It was a principle, a very small principle. I explained to the sergeant that I still had to have a principle—just one small principle.

"India disturbs you," the sergeant agreed sympathetically. "Some people are sensitive about the Far East, and then it disturbs them.''

"Thank you.''

"I mean, I'm sorry it should disturb you this way, because there's so much that's interesting about it.''

"I don't doubt it,'' I said. "When I was in Old Delhi, I used to walk past a factory sometimes, and I noticed that the boys who came off the day shift would gather under a lamp post, and one of them would try to teach the others to read. So I wrote a letter to the commissioner, pointing out how commendable such eagerness for literacy was, and didn't he think he ought to do something about it?''

"He never answered your letter,'' the sergeant said. "Well, neither would Mayor LaGuardia.''

"He answered my letter. He said he was having a stronger bulb put in the lamp post. I suppose you don't believe that?''

"I believe it,'' the sergeant nodded. "It's a funny land, but very interesting, if you're interested in human nature, I mean. If you don't come with me tonight, I got to go anyway, but you can get a jeep and I can't.''

So he stayed to eat with me, and I went with him. The Brass who ate at the Press Club were made uncomfortable by enlisted men at the table—which was understandable—but they never said anything about it, and I knew that sooner or later the sergeant would get better, and they would send him back to putting up telephone wires. I had asked the sergeant how it was that he seemed to know everyone in Calcutta—native people, not Americans or British—and in Bombay and Delhi, and in Rangoon, too, and even as far up north as Yenan; but he only answered that he always made acquaintances, and people were pretty much the same anyway, if you were interested in their problems. "I'm interested in their problems,'' he said.

After dinner, Johnny, who was a native driver, pulled out the jeep, and we got in with two Wire Service men and a Tenth Air Force captain. At that time, the lights were not yet on in Calcutta, even though certain blackout restrictions were being relaxed, and there were still very few street signs; but Johnny knew the city the way you know the palm of your hand, and you just told him where to go and he took you there. We dropped off the other three and then turned into a working-class district of semidetached houses, driving slowly until the sergeant said:

"Here it is."

I told Johnny to return at half past ten, and we walked up the steps of a small stucco building, the kind that are almost a basic unit out there, two entrances and divided into four small three-room apartments. Before we went inside, I asked the sergeant:

"What are these people—reds?"

"What do you mean, reds?"

"I mean, are they Communists?"

"Some are and some aren't. Some of them publish the magazine of the Bengal Literary Society. They're good people, and they want to talk with you."

"It will be a pleasure to talk with them. We're out of bounds, aren't we?"

"Maybe a little."

Then he knocked on the door, and it opened and we went inside, and I wondered how it felt to have your throat out in a dark corner of Calcutta. But after we were inside, I felt better about that, and saw that they were nice people, just as the sergeant had said. Everyone said hello, and then we sat down, and a girl brought us lemonade, and there was a big tray of cookies and sweet candies that looked like orange-colored pretzels. There was also an old electric fan on the ceiling, and that made it not quite so unpleasantly hot as it might have been.

Besides the sergeant and me, there were eight men in the room—the girl went out after she had passed around the drinks—and all but one of them were Indian. The one who wasn't Indian was a British corporal; his name was Hurley, and he had a Cockney accent, and he had behind him a year and a half in Burma. This surprised me a little, because one of the few things I had learned in India was the measure of hatred Indians had for the gentlemen who ruled them. Hurley was a big rosy-cheeked man of about thirty and when he talked, his voice boomed in the place. All of the others spoke softly—in that strangely accented English educated Indians use.

Three of the Indians were trade-unionists, and one of them —as I learned later—was the mass leader of the Bengal workers; it was at his house that we were; the other four were literary men, two of them journalists, two of them teachers at the college. But they all had in common that elemental leanness, the fined-down quality of a people who have not eaten their fill for many, many generations. They were all nice people; they were very gentle people, and they were always thinking of the next thing they would say and framing it so that it would not hurt your feelings. They were glad to have me there, they said; there were many things in India that American news-papermen should see.

I told them I had realized that.

"Mr. Eldridge is sensitive about the East," the sergeant explained, smiling at me apologetically. "Things here disturb him."

Our host, whose name was Charjee, nodded understand-ingly. "Most Americans are disturbed when they come here. It is natural, Mr. Eldridge."

"They get over it," Hurley boomed.

"It's only natural," the sergeant said. "Before the war, the only dead person I ever saw was my grandmother. They're very careful about those things at home. But my friend here had to stay at Lucknow where they have the plague, and there were seven hundred dying each day and nobody to bury them— I mean they laid them out on the road instead, and it's so hot up there—and then he comes down here for the end of the famine—well, you know what I mean."

"But they get over it," Hurley said, and nobody seemed to notice anything out of the way, and no one was embarrassed, except me. I tried to catch the sergeant's eye and express something of what I thought of him, but he was talking to one of the trade-union people, and he wouldn't look my way.

They must have noticed that I wasn't too happy about the trend of the talk, because they shifted over to literary things and they talked about the young writers in India and the struggle for freedom. They had two million men fighting fascism and they said how can you keep a people as slaves who lend two million men to the fight for freedom?

"You're still too gentle," Hurley rushed in. "My word, such a gentle people, you've got to learn different."

A mosquito, hurtled down by the fan, fell on Charjee's knee. He lifted it off and placed it on the floor—he was a Communist too, I learned later—and said, a note of apology in his voice:

"Life is an important thing, and civilized people do not foolishly destroy what is important. Europeans become so annoyed at the cows in our streets—at famine time, I mean." There was a sincere note of regret in his voice.

Hurley said to me: "But make no mistake about it. The cows on the street aren't the whole truth. You haven't begun to understand how complicated it is.''

I was looking around the room with its bare white plaster walls, its straight dark furniture with reed seats, its case of books, its plain grass rug on the floor.

The teacher of English at Calcutta College said, "We would like you to stay for longer than most people stay here, and then perhaps you can write the story about us as it should be written.''

"Mr. Eldridge writes very good,'' the sergeant said. "He should write about you.''

The girl brought in more lemonade, and we talked about the literature of four lands, and they talked with their mouths full of literature—like honey—and properly for a land where five million out of four hundred million can read or write. The girl had long eyes; with her sari draped around her, you couldn't trace her figure, a habit with us, and you had to content yourself with her regal, erect walk. When she walked, Hurley watched her, but there was only a warm contemplation of beauty in his eyes, and it disturbed nobody.

I was not sorry any more that I had come, but only that this strange yet homely evening under the auspices of the Bengal Literary Society was slipping away, and I looked at my watch more frequently.

"He asked the jeep to call for us at half past ten,'' the sergeant explained.

It was a good evening for them too, I think. Charjee shrugged it away.

"Stay and you will have curry with us, and then you can find a rickshaw.''

I shook my head slightly, and the sergeant, glancing sidewise at me, explained that his friend did not ride in rickshaws.

"No? Never?''

Hurley smiled bitterly. The trade-union men looked at each other patiently.

"Could I ask why your friend doesn't ride in rickshaws?" Charjee said politely.

The sergeant explained that I had principles. I felt uncomfortable, because while they were a gentle people, nevertheless men drew them like beasts.

"Principles are fine things to have," Charjee said, "and I respect them." And the teacher of English added, "So many of the Americans have so many principles."

"You see," Hurley said tensely, turning to Charjee, "it isn't so simple with us either." He seemed terribly anxious to be understood.

"Here, in this room, three months ago, we faced a peculiar problem," Charjee said to me, "and I wonder how you would have solved it. It was at the height of the famine, as you may remember, the famine which the British made because they felt that a sick and starving folk would be less of a problem in Bengal. Each morning they picked nine or ten hundred dead bodies off the streets of Calcutta. It was a very bad time, believe me. Well, at the time I speak of, four of us were having dinners here in this room, my daughter, myself, Shogar of the Central Trade-Union Council, and Bose, who is District Party Organizer here. It was not a happy dinner; we had a little rice and a little curry—one meal each day. Well, the window was open, and as we began to eat we heard the cries of the hungry."

"I heard them up the valley," I said. "There was famine there when I came in."

Then you know what I mean. The window was open. That is the problem. What would you have done if you were eating dinner here that night?"

"It is not a fair question," Hurley said, in his incredibly

Cockney accent. "You can't lay his principles alongside of yours."

"I think it's a fair question," I said. "I think I can answer it truthfully enough. I would have given the poor devils my dinner. That isn't heroic or charitable even; I was conditioned that way. Most Americans are."

Hurley smiled again, but there was a sadness in him, a lonely sadness that took the sting from his words. "But they become unconditioned so fast, so very fast. How many thousands of your Americans have I seen here in the East, and almost never did I hear one say Indian, or Burmese, or Chinese, but for all people whose skin is one shade darker than theirs, they have one word, *waug*. They are complicated in their principles, just as my Indian friends are."

"We did not give them our dinner," Charjee said tiredly, as if the evening had suddenly become very long, too long. "We ate our dinner, and in the morning five dead bodies were on my doorstep, two women and three children."

Then there was silence. I didn't know what to say, and nobody else spoke until Charjee continued. "We are a few who will help lead India to freedom, and in this last famine in Bengal five million people died. Those five would have died anyway, a day later, two days later. They will die like that until India is free. There is always a price put on freedom, and part of the price we pay is to stay alive."

Another insect hurtled from the fan to his lap, and without thought he lifted it gently and dropped it to the ground. The sergeant put his hand on my knee and told me:

"You see, Charjee organized the rickshaw drivers. They are a very good union. They are a very militant union. During the past year, they struck three times, and each time they won their gains. They are a very militant union. You see, they haven't much to lose. I mean, the life of a rickshaw driver is only six or eight years after they begin to work, so they haven't much to lose. Some day they will help to do away with rickshaws, but until then—''

The jeep was sounding its horn, and we got up to go. Charjee was afraid he had wounded my feelings—a guest in his house. I must not think that Indians were boors. I must come again, and then we would talk more about literature and he would give me letters to other writers in the States.

"I'll come again," I said. "If you ask me, I'll come again."

"You're not angry?" the sergeant said, when we were in the jeep and on our way.

"Who is Hurley?"—thinking that surely I had met him before and noticing how the gall in him had turned into an almost womanly sweetness as he listened to Charjee.

"He is away from home too long," the sergeant said slowly. "I'm glad I'm not married. He has a wife and two kids and it's four and a half years since he saw them. He is a Communist and was a trade-union leader back home, and they know it, and they keep sending him into Burma and hoping he will be killed."

"He looks healthy."

"I think he'll live," the sergeant said. "The East is very interesting, and if you get used to it, you can stay alive, if you want to enough. Too many people are sensitive about the East."

The Gentle Virtue

THE SERIES OF lectures which Carrol presented during his two-week stay at the University were more of a success than he had anticipated, considering that the subject was "The Inner Ethic of Herman Melville," and at the final convocation he drew a crowd of more than seven hundred, a very singular and unprecedented occurrence.

He had to admit to himself that he had not done badly; four years in the service might have cut him entirely adrift, or it might have had the opposite effect of driving him to the close security of an assistant professorship, both shelter and retreat and a certain amount of dignity too; but he had resisted more successfully than some of his colleagues. He had written and published a book, and he was well on his way with the second one now. To go it alone required more courage than anything he had faced during the war, but he had managed and he would manage, and there was not only relief but a wonderful sense of freedom in the thought that tomorrow he would be returning to New York, to the complicated and variegated world where anything could and did happen. The sense of excitement he experienced whenever he undertook even a minor variation in the course of his life was something he would not willingly surrender; and all things taken together he was, he felt, about as happy as a man could be in these troubled and perturbed United States.

The talk to the convocation was delivered freely and wittily, in a fashion that prompted Madelin Burroughs to tell him, afterwards, that he had a voice that could lull children to sleep, and when he had finished, he managed very well with the few words he had to say to each of the many people, students and faculty and some townspeople, who came crowding around him. A year ago, he would have been terrified and embarrassed by their approach, but he had achieved what he liked to think of as a sort maturity in that time, and it gave him real pleasure to know that there were many people who thought well and warmly of Brighton Carrol.

He was the middle of a small circle; some people came up and introduced themselves and plunged directly into what was on their minds; others held back and waited, and some stood there and smiled at him because they liked him and what he said and the way he looked; and there was one young girl who stood on the edge of the circle watching him, and he could hardly help noticing her, she was so lovely and clean looking. When Professor Andrews drew him away to take him to the reception the English faculty was giving him on this, his last night, he felt a sense of regret that he had not had a chance to talk to the pretty girl. That made it all the better when she was there, getting into Andrews' car with him. They squeezed in with a young instructor, and both were introduced casually by Andrews, who, after he had told Carrol that the girl's name was Lucy Reed, bubbled with praise for the convocation.

"You think," Andrews said; " and you will never know, Brighton, God willing, how rare a quality thought is on a campus."

"Isn't it a new campus though?" Carrol wanted to know.

"Practically everyone I met is a vet."

"That makes a difference," Andrews admitted, and the girl, Lucy Reed, said:

"You haven't met any women, have you?"

Carrol began to apologize, but she took his hand, laughing at him, and then he sat there, uncertain and uneasy about the way she held his hand, uncomfortable too at the overtness of her approach. Yet he couldn't help but feel her assurance, and the almost aggressive approach at him held in it an assured warmth, as if she were an old friend and not someone he had only met this evening. But as they drove along he realized that he had seen her before, at least once, with Andrews, but not noticed her as he was noticing her tonight. He felt, tonight, that fine alertness and sensitivity to life that comes even to the happiest of human beings only once in a while, and then more than makes up for dull days, boredom and frustration. The reception, which would include all of the English faculty, their wives, their petty lusts, jealousies and discontents, he somehow looked forward to with excitement, as if the evening were bound to promise something.

He was not listening to Andrews denying the universality of Melville. "To me, he is a uniquely American product, and it is precisely on that point I'd take issue with you, Brighton." The girl next to him and holding his hand, he discovered, was more than handsome and quite beautiful, pale, but with fine, clean-cut features and a long-limbed body. His own reserve, he finally decided, qualified everything; that was one of the reasons he remained unmarried at thirty-five; that was why, if the evening were not otherwise so pleasant, he would have resented fiercely Andrews, whom he hardly knew, a professor in Elizabethan Poetry, calling him by his first name and plunging on with an obviously ridiculous criticism. Andrews didn't know what he was talking about, but that he dismissed with an offhand remark and spoke to the girl, but only a few words. Then they were there, looking for a parking place outside of the department head's house.

"You will be lionized tonight," the girl said.

Andrews told him, as they got out of the car, "We can get away at twelve, if you just want to sit down at my place and relax, my wife and perhaps one or two others."

He answered noncommittally, more annoyed with Andrews because the girl had slipped away and gone into the house than because Andrews' invitation was not in the best of taste. However, he liked Andrews' wife, whom he remembered as a pleasant, healthy-looking woman who had sat through one of his seminars, and he substituted "I'll see" for a straight refusal.

Inside, everyone had liked his talk at the convocation and told him so, and he reflected again that this was a department in which he would work very comfortably and perhaps with a good deal of satisfaction. There was something large and straightforward about Carrol, and he had that easy youthfulness which is characteristic of many American men, and which, when combined with any degree of intelligence, can be immensely charming. Also, early in his stay at the University, he had endeared himself to the English faculty.

The head of the department had a pleading, Middle Western passion for Wordsworth, which he indulged to the extent of spending all of the department's museum money on first editions of the British bard. Aside from resentment on national grounds, there were other poets who ranked higher in the estimation of various membrs of the department, and their joy knew no bounds when Carrol said to the head, at lunch one day:

"I should think it would be Riley."

"Who?"

"Instead of Wordsworth, I mean."

"Did you say Riley?"

Innocently enough and without smiling, Carrol managed, "Yes, James Whitcomb Riley. I mean, he trod this very soil—"

The head of the department never quite made up his mind whether Carrol was a Philistine or a boor, but the story was told around, and everyone else loved him for it. Now, tonight, they were genuinely sorry that he was going away, and the group of animated men and women, drinking sherry and brandy, almost took on that warm and wise and balanced combination of wit and civilization that had become so foreign to America, but still lurked on a campus. Or it may have been that Carrol wanted to see it that way and did. In any case, he was at his best, and they talked of what he felt were better things than war and the threat of war, the ugly, crouching monster which implied that this was the end of all things for all time.

Lucy Reed sat near him, but not obtrusively. She would move away and then be back again, watching him. When he had a minute alone with Eve Andrews, he asked her, "How old is the Reed girl?"

"Why?"

"I thought I'd like to know something about her—what she does. Is she on the staff?"

"She's twenty-nine. She was after her doctorate, but gave it up."

And he was moved to say lamely that he thought she looked younger. It was the way Mrs. Andrews regarded him that thrust him away, and he found himself listening to the conversation instead of being a part of it, and thereby it became commonplace, a good deal of it rather stupid. He listened to people saying things to him, and he answered them too, but an insa-

tiable loneliness had suddenly taken hold of him; and he wondered whether in a foolish, adolescent way, he was forming a
crush for Lucy Reed. It would be ironic, indeed, he told himself,
if after waiting as long as he had—incapable for some reason
that had never troubled him overmuch of forming a permanent
alliance or relationship with any woman—he were to form what
he liked to think of as a fixation on a girl in a provincial Middle
Western college town.

But he forgot that when he found a few minutes alone
with her and they were able to talk. She was quite tall, a strong,
long-limbed girl, and in the way she stood, her actions, her
speech—in everything about her, actually—was that quality
he envied so much, a fierce devotion to life, a love of life, a
consuming interest in the very essence of living. There was no
cynicism in her, yet obtuseness was not there as a substitute.
She seemed to be better read and better informed than most
of the people he had met on the campus, and she looked at him
with the kind of alert delight that he had not found in the eyes
of any woman in a long, long time.

"I like you," she said to him. "I do wish I had met you
when you first came."

"Would it make much difference?"

"Of course it would," she said. "In a world as rotten and
as beautiful as this one, you are a rare, good person."

"How do you know?"

"What did you do in the war?" she asked him.

"I was an infantryman."

"And it didn't affect you, and you came back to Herman
Melville. Now I've hurt you."

"You haven't hurt me," he said, enormously contained.

"Only I wish I could have seen what you saw and been
through what you were through."

"Why?"

"You don't know why, do you?" she asked him curiously.

"Couldn't we get away from here?" he wanted to know. "Couldn't I buy you a beer and couldn't we sit down and talk?"

"Why?" she smiled.

"This is not getting us anywhere, is it?" Carrol said. "I have my ticket on the nine o'clock plane in the morning. I would like to spend an hour with you."

"That's flattering."

"No—you know what I mean to say."

"I don't, really, but I'll see you at the Andrewses' later, won't I?"

"Will you be there?"

"Of course I will. I live there."

"You live there?"

"I'm the professor's adopted daughter—didn't you know?"

She said it seriously, yet he took it as an awkward jest, and reinforced himself, as he always had, with the failings of others. She was not as bright as he had thought, and having already projected, in an indulgent and inward way, as he had with so many other women—projected but never consummated—a situation in which he followed his fancy, fell completely in love, married, lived his life, he found it neither attractive nor hopeful. And as if she had read his mind, she looked at him almost pityingly before she turned away.

He wanted to speak to her again, but did not have a chance to until much later. Instead, his eyes followed her, wherever she was in the room, picking her up again and again and sometimes meeting her eyes and sometimes finding her smiling at him. Only a part of his mind was in the conversations he fell into here and there. The most of him was with her now in a warm, petulant desire; and while he talked about literature, campus gossip, and the war too, he was erecting in his mind the mechanism whereby he might find time alone with her that evening to at least have a stab at making love. He forced the substitution of a night with her for that endless span which a man had to consider once he admitted to himself that he could love a woman and that perhaps she could love him. Yet he couldn't help wondering what that remark about being the adopted daughter of Andrews meant, feeling at the same time a wave of resentment against Andrews for the fact that she lived with him. His own casualness in terms of any man-woman relationship had long ago convinced him that cohabitation inevitably followed proximity, and the possibility of some sordid triangle within Andrews' home sickened him. More curiously than before, he studied Andrews, a matter-of-fact academic type, in his late thirties, sandy-haired, spectacled, civilized to the high impotence of those few cloistered and cultured beings America boasts, and vegetating quietly in a Middle Western university.

At about eleven o'clock, when the reception showed signs of breaking up, Carrol sought out Lucy Reed and reminded her. "I have my car outside," she said, "and if you can manage to slip away, I'll take you home with me—if you want to come?"

"To Andrews' place?"

"Yes. Won't you come? After two hours of talking to fifty people, I should imagine you'd like to sit down and talk with two or three."

"Or one," said Carrol.

She shook her head, and Carrol said, all right, he'd find some way to get out.

"The car is a little, beat-up Ford coupe," she said. "I left it at the corner under the lamp post before the convocation, and it's probably still there.''

"In ten minutes," Carrol said optimistically.

He saw no reason to be secretive about it, and he told Eve Andrews that Lucy was driving him over to their place. "All right," she said. "It's nice that you can come." Then he made his excuses, said his good-bys, and got out into the cool spring air. That finished it, and he was glad to be away. It had taken something to get out of there alone, and they would talk about it, but he didn't much care. He found the car, with Lucy already in it, and there was almost a note of casual old acquaintanceship in the way they nodded at each other. She drove to the Andrewses' place in a roundabout route that took them past the edge of an old limestone quarry, filled with a placid pool of water that shimmered gently in the fine moonlight. Feeling that he was expected to kiss her, Carrol tried; she didn't resist, and then he couldn't do anything more than sit beside her lonely and quiet and disturbed until they reached the Andrewses', thinking of what she would say if he blundered out that he loved her, even though he knew nothing more about her or who she was or where she came from or where she thought she was going.

At the Andrewses', aside from the professor and his wife, there was just an amiable young instructor from the law school. There was a good fire in the old-fashioned living room, and they all sat in front of it, drinking bourbon and soda, and talking that kind of literary talk Carrol loved better than anything else. When Carrol remarked, "I'm afraid I took the edge off the reception, bolting out like that," Andrews observed that the host and hostess were probably everlastingly indebted to him for ending it so early. They made no further reference to his impending departure, but Carrol was conscious by now of their liking for him, a strange liking that was tinged, at least

on the part of Eve Andrews, with a curiosity he hardly understood. If it had not been for the very naturalness and warmth
of this late evening gathering, he might have sensed something
terrible and impending; but how could he when the conversation flowed so normally and well?

They talked about the ten best tales that men had written,
and then, enthralled, as people whose work is literature will be,
by the process of storytelling and storymaking, they traced the
lines of development through many lands and cultures. That
kind of talk, Carrol reflected, can be in this world a sort of wine,
gentle and civilized, heart-warming and soul-comforting, re-
claiming as it does what man has achieved and not what he has
destroyed. At first Carrol had to fight down a sort of childish
resentment against the young law school instructor, but everything he said and did made it self-evident that he was no more
than a good friend to Lucy Reed, while everything Lucy Reed
did and said made it plainly apparent to Carrol, if not to everyone else there, that he was a special quality with her. With no
self-consciousness, innocently as a small girl, she gave her heart
to him, and he would have had to be insensitive indeed not
to feel it and respond to it. Withal, she was so easily a part of
the group that Carrol found himself completely unable to
fathom what relationship she bore to the others.

That they loved her was obvious, but the quality and
nature of the love only puzzled Carrol. He habitually made
the mistake of so many intellectuals, that of oversimplifying
people whom he considered of lesser capacity, and he found
himself revising his estimate of Professor Andrews and his wife
—and his estimate of Lucy Reed too. Watching her pale, clean-
cut, lovely face in the shadows of the firelight, he became more
and more convinced that the seemingly aimless flow of events
had paused meaningfully as it brought them together, and as

the early morning began, he no longer denied to himself that he was completely and wonderfully in love.

During the decade past, he would have strongly and reasonably denied the spirituality of love, the selflessness and wonder of it, and now he accepted it wholly and felt as so many others have felt, that he suddenly was different from and beyond all other human beings. The imminence of age, which only lately had come to prey upon him and bedevil him, turned into a flower of youth, and the youthfulness became a bond between them. His whole future suddenly had turned and fixed upon a woman, and between fragments of conversation, he made plans. He would go to New York, even as he was scheduled to, but in a week at the most he would be back here. He might live and work here for a while; the place would not only be bearable, but charming. After all, he told himself, the attitude which led him to reject this place was a manufactured sophistication; had he not told himself a hundred times, during the war, that any corner of America could be wonderful?

That way, his thoughts roved along, and suddenly it was past one in the morning. Lucy Reed rose and said abruptly:

"I'm very tired. Will you excuse me?"

Carrol got up and took her warm hand in his. "Good night," she said. She left then and Carrol heard her going upstairs. The evening was over now, and Eve Andrews, catching his eye, said, "I'll drive you home whenever you're ready to go, Brighton."

"What about a nightcap?" the professor asked. "One more small one."

The law school instructor stretched his arms and yawned, and at that moment, while Eve Andrews emptied an ash tray into a silent butler, Carrol heard the noise—a harsh grating human noise. Someone was moaning or calling aloud in pain, he thought, but no one else appeared to notice it. The noise came again, and he started and demanded:

"Didn't you hear it? What was that?"

"Lucy," Eve Andrews said shortly. Suddenly the professor and the law school instructor were contemplatively silent, absorbed in their drinks.

After a long moment, Carrol said, "What do you mean, Lucy?"

"She's ill. She has difficulty keeping anything on her stomach."

"She doesn't look sick," Carrol said. "What is it—an ulcer?"

"It's worse than an ulcer," Eve Andrews said quietly. "It's a kind of cancer called 'Hodgkin's disease.' "

"Is it bad?"

The professor asked shortly, almost angrily, "How bad can cancer be?"

Driving Carrol back to the Grand Union, where he had boarded during his stay at the University, Eve Andrews was strangely unresponsive to Carrol's horror. "It happens," she said, almost coldly. "And her family couldn't face it. They couldn't deal with it. Every night the girl went to bed with mortal fear that she wouldn't wake in the morning. She's better since she came to live with us."

"When—" Carrol began.

"Six months ago was the date they set."

"But she doesn't look sick or act sick."

"That's right."

"And isn't there anything to hope for?" Carrol pleaded.

"A miracle—if you believe in them."

"No cure, no method . . .?"

"No cure, that's right."

"No, it can't be," Carrol said. "Not that beautiful, wonderful girl. It can't be."

Eve Andrews shrugged, and Carrol turned on her fiercely and demanded, "How in hell can you be so cold about it?"

"Do you think I'm cold about it?" she said tiredly. "I grew up with Lucy. I'm a year older than she. We played together as kids and then we had dates together. Now we try to make the little bit left normal and worthwhile. You don't want to face that, do you? Were you falling in love with her before you found this out?"

When he didn't answer, she went on. "What have you ever faced? You saw no death in the war, did you? You don't live in a world where people are born and where they die."

"That's a hell of a thing to say."

"What do you want me to say? Did you see her eyes tonight? Suppose you had a day or three days or three weeks to live? There's a good deal of nonsense talked about love, but there's something else about love too—or maybe you don't know?"

They had drawn up before the Grand Union now, and for a minute or two, they sat there in silence. Then Eve Andrews said, "Good night, Brighton."

"Good night," Carrol said.

Carrol spent a sleepless night. It was not until sunrise that he understood how foolish a quixotic action can be. It was not until sunrise that he could blend peace and pity with a calm understanding that grown men did not fall in love in that fashion. He told himself that he would always remember Lucy Reed with pity and affection; and he also told himself that the quick image he had conceived the night before of marrying a girl in such a position was hardly sensible and beneficial surely to neither.

A few hours later he was boarding his plane, reflecting, as he so often did, on the virtues of a civilized man in a basically uncivilized world.

Dumb Swede

TOM ANDERSON HAD not been born in the old country, but growing up on the farm among Swedish and Norwegian folk gave him a slight accent that for some reason persisted all his life. He was not very quick with his tongue or his thoughts and perhaps that was what preserved the accent. Sometimes, also, he thought that this same slowness accounted for the fact that he never learned to read or write; while it was true that he had no schooling, ever, again and again he met people without schooling who had learned to read. He never learned, just as he never learned to remove the quality from his speech that marked him as a Swede.

Certainly, he had been around enough. He was eleven years old when he left the farm to work at the mill, and there he spent three years with the taste of flour always in his mouth, flour in his clothes, in his hair, and in every crevice of his skin. How he hated flour, the taste of it, the smell of it, the stinging burn of it! But in those three years he grew a full twelve inches; he broadened out, and at fourteen he was able to heave two hundred-pound sacks onto his back and carry them with ease. When he was able to do that, he figured he was able to take care of himself, and he told the mill operator, Ole Svenson:

"I'm going away now and get a job pays better than four

dollars a week''—a speech he had rehearsed slowly and carefully
for at least ten days.

"You stay here, or your old man'll beat your hide off,"
Svenson said.

"My old man can go to hell, and you too," Tom Anderson
replied, and with that he shook the mill dust out of his clothes
and set out on the dirt road that led north through the wheat
fields.

Often enough afterwards, in the years that followed, Tom
Anderson thought of that day, and sometimes he regretted that
he had walked off that way, with never a word of sweetness or
departure to his mother and father. But neither had he ever had
a good word from them, only beatings and blows as one of seven
children, and turned out to work when he was eleven, and not
a day of schooling in his life. Stupid he was, as they told him
often enough, and schooling was for those with brains—although
he never understood the logic of that. So while he regretted his
leave-taking, he did not regret it too much, nor was he given
to brooding about it overmuch.

At seventeen, he had three years of work in the lumber
camps behind him, and he stood six feet and two inches in his
stockings, weighed one hundred and ninety pounds, and could
use an ax and a saw as well as the next man. The women he
saw, the bad women who lived around the camps, in the little
towns near by, thought he was older than he was and considered
him very handsome, what with his light blue eyes, his sandy
hair, and his broad, even-featured face. But they also thought
him stupid, not knowing his age and the fact that he had known
no other women before them. The reputation they gave him as
a "dumb Swede" spread through the camps, and because Tom
Anderson was slow-going and good-natured, it was never
seriously contested. There were other factors too. Most of the

men spent their spare time reading Western magazines or Nick Carter novels; Tom Anderson could not read, but he was ashamed to admit it to anyone; he bought a corncob pipe, learned to smoke it, and spent hours just sitting and doing nothing in particular, except smoking his pipe. Because he was big and strong, he avoided fights; if prodded into one, he usually did well enough.

Then the work in the lumber camps fell off, and men were laid off right and left. A Wobbly organizer appeared, and some of the men listened to him and others didn't. Tom Anderson didn't. Ever since he had worked in the flour mill and earned four dollars a week, two of which were given over to his father and two of which he paid back for room and board, he had been jealous of the wages he made. Now the Wobblies seemed to threaten his right to work as he pleased, and he talked against them. He had been laid off, but the straw boss hired him back on at five dollars more a month. It was all right for a while, but then a bunch of the men ganged up on him and gave him an awful beating. Strangely enough, he didn't hold the beating against them, nor was that the reason he pulled out. He had never really been very much afraid of anything, and he would not have been afraid to take another beating if he had to. It was just that he was sick and tired of lumbering, and he thought if he were to make a new start somewhere else, maybe people would act differently toward him and he would get away from the business of being a ''dumb Swede.''

He caught a string of boxcars south, and for the next five years he drifted from job to job, from Minneapolis to St. Louis to El Paso to San Francisco and Seattle. But everywhere it was the same, and wherever he went, they caught on sooner or later to the fact that he was just a big dumb Swede. Anderson was a good worker, and even if he had money in his pocket, he couldn't stay idle. The need for work, the drive for work was deeply imbedded within him. Almost since he could remember now, the principal avocation and expression of his life was in work with his hands.

He had the large, square, beautiful hands of big-boned, hard-working men. He didn't know it, of course. He met a girl once, just a girl in a house, who looked at his hands and saw a little of what Rodin or Epstein would have seen in them, and her face lit up; but she didn't know how to put it into words and you don't tell a big, blond squarehead that his hands are beautiful. She stared at his hands until he asked her what she was looking at, and then she said:

"Nothing, nothing at all."

But for a long time afterwards she remembered those hands.

Anderson never became much of a drinker. He didn't like the stuff, and when he had a pile, most of it went on women. Moving from job to job, the steel mills, a cannery, the railroad, the stockyards, reaping, picking fruit, pick and shovel, pouring concrete, a cowcamp—moving along that way, he never met any girls that he could just get to know and go around with. Women lived in a *house;* that was the begining and the end of it for him.

This wasn't good, and one time, working on a right of way in Idaho, he met up with another Swede, Jack Orlaffson, a man of about fifty who had been born in the old country. Tom Anderson never made many friends, because he was the sort of open-handed young fellow who could be taken advantage of too easily, and so many were willing to make a mark of him that there was hardly any opening for someone to make a friend of him. But Orlaffson took a real and sincere liking to him. Anderson was twenty-three years old, and Orlaffson told him that he ought to think of settling down.

"You been a working man," Orlaffson said to him. "You get a dollar and you spend a dollar. But how many fellows like you I see been working men, been just a bum sooner or later."

"I never been without a job," Tom Anderson said.

"Well, you just wait until hard times come. You listen to me, you get a nice girl. Get a family. A man got nothing in world outside a family."

"Where am I going to find a nice girl?" Tom Anderson wondered.

"Just look around you, I tell you, and you see a nice girl all right. You see one."

So Tom Anderson looked around him, but since most of the places he was outside of the job were whorehouses, beer halls, and dance halls, he didn't see many nice girls. Then the right of way was finished, and he and Orlaffson went to Butte, where they worked in a mine.

Here again, Tom Anderson ran into the Wobblies. They came into Butte to work on copper, and Anderson's mistrust was shared by Orlaffson. "They got nothing for us," Orlaffson said. "They're crazy as hell with strike, strike, strike—all the time." Orlaffson had two children with his mother-in-law in Omaha; a widower, he sent every penny he made there. When the Wobblies sent a deputation of three big Swedes to talk with Anderson and Orlaffson, Orlaffson shook his head stubbornly:

"I never been a union man—I don't be one now."

"I don't be one," said Anderson. "I look after myself." Which was strange, because he was a mark for anyone who was broke two days after pay day, or who had a sob story to tell him.

"Okay," they said. "Okay—you big dumb Swede. We see you today and tomorrow you'll be out there scabbing."

But when the strike broke, both Orlaffson and Anderson pulled out and went to Chicago. Neither of them wanted trouble; they just wanted to work and hold down their jobs. But there were bad times in Chicago then, and in the rest of America too. Orlaffson felt it more than Anderson; Anderson was strong as an ox, and he could find certain kinds of work when they turned away anyone past forty, regardless of strength. All that cold, long winter, Anderson gave his friend money. To a degree, he adopted Orlaffson's two children as his own responsibility, and twice he scabbed so that he could earn money for the two children he had never seen. Orlaffson was very grateful, and Tom Anderson was happy that he had found a real friend.

Then Tom Anderson found a steady job in the big harvester plant and he found a girl. Never in this wildest dreams would he have hoped for that kind of girl. She had yellow hair that was like fine, spun-metal wire, and she had beautiful red lips and lovely features. She had a sensuous, full figure, and Tom Anderson considered her the most beautiful creature he had ever seen. Her name was Jane Bogan, and she affectionately called Anderson "my big, beautiful dumb Swede." She was beautiful and she called him beautiful! He met her in a dance hall, and a week later they were married. After that, he introduced her to Orlaffson. The older man was nice to her, but she called him "Pop" and said later to Anderson:

"So that's your friend! Why he's a worse squarehead than you are!"

Anderson tried to explain, but he was not nimble enough with words to say what he felt for Orlaffson. The older man was still not working steadily, but Jane wouldn't hear of giving him money.

"How much does he owe you now?" she asked Anderson.

"I don't know—I don't keep track."

"You mean you been feeding that squarehead for a year and you didn't keep track of it?"

"That's right," Anderson said miserably, feeling that she knew, finally and forever, what a complete fool he was. He never blamed her for anything after that, but went around immersed in his own guilt. At first, they had a fine bodily relationship, but that finished after she became pregnant and got some medicine from the druggist to purge herself with. She wouldn't go near him after that, and Anderson was so miserable he couldn't sleep, couldn't eat, and went through his motions at work like an automation. He went to Jack Orlaffson with his troubles, but Orlaffson only shrugged his shoulders. Orlaffson had plenty of his own troubles.

Then Orlaffson went back to Omaha, and that was the last Anderson ever saw of him. It was a real blow to Anderson; he had never had a friend like Jack Orlaffson before; he never hoped to have one again. Orlaffson was the only person who had never called him a dumb Swede, who seemed to understand him; Orlaffson was the only person he had ever been able to talk to.

His wife was pleased. "It's about time you shook that squarehead," she said.

And for that he had no answer. He had thought that marriage meant a home and children, but after the second year, Jane didn't bother being home when he arrived. He ate in restaurants or he prepared his own food, and even when some of the men in the plant told him that they had seen his wife here and there, drinking and dancing, he didn't have the heart to talk about it, she was so beautiful and smart, and he such a dumb Swede!

So it went, for three years, and then he came home one night and found a note from her. The note said that she was

going away to New York. She liked him, it said, but there was
no use remaining together, because they were so obviously
unsuited for each other. It took a long while for him to work
up enough courage to go next door to the Grahams and ask
them to read the note. He was not only ashamed of being
illiterate, but he was ashamed and frightened of what he suspected would be in the note.

After he heard the note read, he cried for the first time in
many years. All his life he would miss her and go on wondering
how he had ever been married to anything so lovely. Yet what
she said was true; he didn't hate her either. It was just that
they were unsuited to each other. He didn't think of a divorce,
because he didn't know much about divorces or how people
went about obtaining them; and down underneath he retained
a faint hope that she would return to him.

Yet he couldn't go back to randying like a young colt—
even if he had wanted to, which he didn't particularly. He
stayed on the same job for another six months, and then he
drifted on to Cleveland. In Cleveland, he worked at a steel
mill, and alongside of him were two Poles who had a sister.
They evidently looked upon him as a marriage prospect, taking
him home with them, and making it easy for him and the sister
to be together. But when they found out subsequently that
Tom Anderson was married, they became very angry and threatened to beat the hell out of him.

Anderson couldn't stay still. Cleveland to St. Louis to New
Orleans, where he shipped out. It was the time before America's
entry into the First World War, when the U-boats were just
beginning to operate on a large scale, and there were berths
in plenty for men who wanted to ship. Anderson made three
trips to Europe before America entered the war, and then for
some reason he never quite understood, he enlisted. Maybe it

was the parades and the banners and the posters, which pointed such accusing fingers at him. Whatever it was, he went in, and was put in the engineers, where his big hands found work to do. Nothing changed much. He was still the big dumb Swede, and he dug ditches, laid spur lines, and poured concrete. He never got to Europe, and when the war was over, he had eleven dollars in his pocket and an army uniform on his back.

It was at that time that a great longing to see Orlaffson came over him. He had thought first of going to New York City and attempting to find his wife, Jane; but he realized that New York was a big place and he suspected that Jane would have no use for him, even if he found her. During the war, he had been with this woman and that one, and there had even been a nice Croatian girl in Pittsburgh, where he had been stationed for a while, who had wanted to marry him. But no girl actually took the place of Jane, even partly; and he decided he would make his way out to Omaha on the freights and see Orlaffson instead. He wasn't so young any more, and he had a touch of rheumatism in his back when the weather was bad, and the heavy veins on his arms and hands were harder and higher than ever before. He thought that Orlaffson might ask him to stop by for a while and maybe live with him and the children. It didn't occur to him at all that in the years since he had seen Orlaffson the children would have grown up, and that by now Orlaffson, if alive, would have been quite an old man.

To his surprise, he discovered that there were a good many Orlaffsons in Omaha, none of whom had the first name of Jack. That left him nothing else to do but go from door to door, since now that he had come all the way to Omaha, he was determined to find his friend. He spent a whole day in that fashion, a big, broad-shouldered, rawboned Swede with sparse sandy hair, ringing bells and inquiring:

"Please, is there Jack Orlaffson, a friend of mine, living here?"

It was a time when folks were nervous about ex-servicemen, so many of whom didn't have jobs; so they should not be thought of too harshly, those who were short and snappish with Anderson. At the same time, it surprised him to learn that there were Orlaffsons so prosperous and others so poor in Omaha. There was one family in a great, beautiful mansion that looked like the governor's house itself, and there was another in a stick and tar-paper shack down by the yards. But none of them was the Orlaffson he sought.

Finally, on toward evening, he rang the bell of an apartment. A nice girl answered the door, a healthy, good-looking young girl, and behind her a baby gurgled and the smell of cooking food filled the air.

"Jack Orlaffson?" she said. "What do you want of him?"

"My name is Tom Anderson, and he was my friend."

"So you're Tom Anderson," she said, very warmly. "Jack was my father-in-law, and I remember how he used to talk about you, but my goodness, the old man's been dead since before the war."

With a rush and a roar and a hammer, time descended upon Tom Anderson. For so long, the years had stood still! Now they all descended upon him with a great rush and roar until his head spun and he thought his senses would leave him.

It was not so much the fact of Orlaffson's death, although afterwards that would grieve him a good deal; death he was used to; but it was the way this young girl spoke of his friend, as an old man who belonged to the far, far past. It was the way, all of a sudden, the years fled past that left him so bereft and lonely and unhappy.

The young girl looked at him with sympathy, and asked

him wouldn't he come in and have a cup of tea and a piece of cake?

"No," he said dully—"no, I got to go somewhere else."

Afterwards, she told her husband about it and remarked, "I felt so sorry for the poor dumb Swede."

After that, for Anderson, time seemed to race, as if some incredible brake had been removed. The only part that paused, even comparatively, was three months he spent in jail, during the Palmer Raids, when he had been mistaken for an alien because of the slight accent that still lingered. He had been picked up in a saloon with a crowd of workers; it was the first real trouble he ever got into, and when, finally, after three months, he was brought to trial, he got out easily enough. But it added to his old, old mistrust of unions and radicals: reasoning that if not for them and their activities, none of this trouble would have started.

Bad times came, and for two years he had only occasional jobs. It was no longer easy, as it had once been, to take the roughest and dirtiest work and laugh it off. More frequently, his back hurt; more frequently, he woke up with a stiff neck, with every joint throbbing in pain. And now, for the first time, he found himself being passed by while younger men got the jobs.

Still, he was a good worker, and when he landed a job in a paper mill outside of St. Paul, he kept it a full five years. During a part of that time, he lived with a widow who kept a boardinghouse; but he never felt any real closeness to her, and the relationship was one that simply dwindled away. More and more often now, he regretted that he had never learned to read; reading, he felt, could put a brake on time passing; reading might give him something to hold on to. He went to the movies a good deal, but unless the story could be followed without the subtitles, he was confused and disturbed.

There was no itemizing the years. One became very much like another. The paper mill closed down with the crash, and Tom Anderson took to the road again. It seemed only yesterday that there were bad times, but here they were again, such times as no man had ever dreamed of before. The whole world was on the road now, moving, drifting, scrabbling for the bones.

It's one thing to go on the road when you're seventeen or twenty-five years old; it's another thing to go on the road when fifty is just ahead of you. It's one thing to nose out the next man when you can put in two hours to his one; it's another thing for them to tell you, *nothing doing, Pop, nothing doing.*

Yet a force drove him. He was a worker; he had always been a worker—why else then had God given him two strong hands? He had to work. If he didn't work, he didn't live. If he didn't work, he might just as well stop living. He might just as well lie down on the earth and breathe out his life.

He lived, without comprehending why; he found jobs here and there, and time passed. He went into a town where a steel mill was opening and he stood a whole day in line until it was his turn, and then they said to him, *nothing doing, Pop.* In Los Angeles, he worked as a cleaning man in a dance hall.

"What do you pay?" he had asked them.

They took one look at the big, dumb Swede and they answered, "Thirty a month and meal at night," and he took it because he had to live.

He was not old, he tried to tell himself, thinking of all the stories of the old country where a round span of life was eighty, and a hundred was not out of the question. He sat in a moving picture house—better now because the pictures were accompanied by sound—and found himself gauging the age of the actors. So many of them must be as old as he was, and yet

there they were, loving women, having adventures and ro-
mances, and consistently making fortunes, so they could live
in their wonderful palaces. In a way, it gave him heart, but his
high spirits always vanished when he came out into the cold air
of reality.

After the dance hall, he worked as a male chambermaid in
a dirty old flophouse in Denver. He stuck to that for almost a
year, hating it and despising himself for being there, but deep-
stricken now with the fear of not finding another job and being
in the place of the poor, gray-skinned devils who made this
their home. Yet eleven months of bitter, senile emasculation
was all he could stomach. He was an industrial worker; when he
looked at his two hands, still so strong and large, still retaining
the form of their old beauty, his heart became sick with remembering the things they had built. He was a worker who built,
who drained, who created, who fed the vitals of those great
piles called plants; what was he doing here in this awful place?

He rode east to Chicago, where many wheels were turning
with the pressure of an approaching war, and in Chicago he
went from plant to plant. What couldn't he do? Where had
he not worked? Did they want a machinist, a turret operator,
a butcher, a stoker, a drop forger, a metal cutter—well, he
was each and all of them.

"Maybe you were once, Pop," they told him, feeling sorry
in their hearts, some of them, for the big, shambling man.

When at last he had to eat, he took a job as doorman in
one of those magnificent houses that face the lake on the Near
North Side. The guts of the struggle gone now, he gave in, and
all day long he opened the door and closed it, helped people
out of cars and into them, whistled for taxis and carried bundles.

The years fled now. In his room, Tom Anderson tried to
cling to those last muttering years; he installed a radio, listened

to Munich, heard the rumble of war again and the tale of the invasion of Norway. Most of it he did not understand, any more than he had understood or responded to the great organizational surges of the thirties, when the CIO was born. But war he hated, and he felt himself moved as he had never been moved before. Norwegians he hated too, because when he was a little child, it was thought right that a Swede should hate Norwegians, yet he wept as he listened to the tales out of Norway.

His back pained him more and more, as the days fled. His hair turned white, and the seasons passed while he opened and closed the door. He was an old man. One morning, his back pained him so that he could not rise, and he lay in bed weeping with fear and frustration. Somehow, the next day, he dragged himself to work. He had never been sick before; it was more terrible than he had ever imagined it would be to be a sick old man.

"You got to keep up with the job, Tom," the superintendent told him, "I know how it is, but you got to keep up with the job," thinking that perhaps it would be better to get rid of the dumb Swede now instead of later.

"I keep up," Anderson promised. "I swear I do."

A great and fearful emptiness had opened within him, and in the black depths of his desperation he recalled that his folks had been Lutheran—and he went to the Lutheran Church one Sunday. But it gave him neither peace nor comfort; he had been too long away and he did not want prayer, but the right to work and the dignity of it.

The war went on and the war finished. Everyone in the house and everyone who visited there knew old Tom Anderson, but no one ever thought of him as a man or as a human fellow with human hopes and woes, but only as another part of the tall, shiny building, like the doors and the elevators and the canopy outside.

Everyone said, "Hello, Tom—what do you know?" But no one cared what he knew.

The pain in his back was worse than ever now. On some days, the pain seemed to permeate his entire body, and it became more and more of a torture to drag himself from bed in the morning. Again, he was away from work for three days, and this time the superintendent really made up his mind to replace him. But after that, for five months, Tom Anderson managed to show up each day, and the superintendent relented a little.

But Tom Anderson knew he could not keep it up long. The strength of his big body was going; he lost flesh, and the pain became worse and worse, until one morning he woke fitfully, the pain coming and going in undulating waves, driving him from consciousness back to unconsciousness. Then he knew he was going to die. Here he was, an old man alone in this furnished room, with no one to call out for and no one to help him, and he was dying.

An anger came to him now that was unlike any anger he had ever experienced before. His life was gone; it had rolled away like a shadow and it was over, and he had nothing, not kith nor kin nor a place he could call his own. All through the years, he had been a good worker, a strong worker, a faithful worker, but no one cared and it mattered to no one. Fury raged all through him, but the fury could not be directed anywhere because he knew of no place or target to direct it upon. He was bereft, yet he knew not of what he was bereft. His old eyes shed tears, but the tears were in vague and hopeless groping for all the roads he had not traveled and would never travel.

And presently, those thoughts became confused and meaningless, and in what remained of his consciousness there was only a flicker of himself as a poor, dumb Swede, whose life was like a formless shadow.

The Gray Ship

WITH WORK WELL done, the gray ship lay in the eastern sunshine and slept. Moored to the dockside with heavy hawsers, fore and aft, she was as immobile as part of the earth, the dock, the rusty, war-weary storage sheds. She had come halfway around the world, her holds stuffed with the food and the teeth of war, her decks piled; she had threaded her way through the islands and atolls of the Pacific, crawled around the belly of Australia, crept lightless and soundless through the tropical night. She was sufficient to herself; when her engines broke down, she hove to and repaired them; when danger threatened, she manned her guns and slewed them belligerently to the part of the horizon which menaced her. She had been a living, vibrating world, rusty and hard; now she was painted over from head to foot, and she lay in the sunshine and slept.

The purser was nervous; big, heavy, his usual smile gone, he stood by the rail, drummed his fingers on the hot metal, and wanted to be away. That nervousness had communicated itself to the whole crew; longing for port, talking port, dreaming it, when it came it was always less than it should have been, and when port time ran over schedule they became restless and uneasy. And this they tried to cover over by pointing out that their pay went on, good pay in this, a danger zone.

"It stinks," the purser said. He meant it literally; in the basin, the garbage could not be thrown overside; it littered the aft deck, mixed indiscriminately with the dunnage. A ship in port, loading or unloading, isn't clean. Crows screamed and cawed and swooped over the garbage. Flies made a netting over it.

"A dead ship," the purser said. "She sleeps, she lays on her belly like a whore. I don't like a ship that way." He begun to hum, "Don't fence me in—give me land." The chief came up and joined his music; the chief's eyes wandered from the burnished metal skies to the ship, to the crows. Of the crows, he asked, "What are they?" "Crows." "I don't like crows," the chief said. "I don't like crows by the hundreds. I liked to hear them way off across the meadows at home, but not like this. What's new?"

The purser said he didn't know wht was new, and anyway, what should be new? The chief thought that maybe he had some news on where they were going, but the purser only grunted. But inside, momentarily, he had a quick, wide thought: fifteen thousand miles from stateside, the whole world was theirs, its waters washing motes of land, unimportant land, wretched, hot land: he had a sudden sense of freedom, and he pitied the army guards, seeking shade under the rusty shed, he pitied the natives of the land who were like the trees, rooted to the land.

"I want to hear the turbines," he said.

"You want to hear the turbines," the chief muttered. "The rotten noisiest can I ever been on, and you want to hear it. You got bugs in your head."

"When the engines turn over, she's alive; now she's dead.

A ship without power, she's dead.''

"We ought to have a funeral service," the chief said; but the purser, pouring ample quantities of sweat, drummed with his fingers on the rail and wanted to be away.

The gray ship was a Victory, which meant that whatever her given name, it would be followed by the word "Victory," as, for instance, the *Arkansas Victory* or the *Burnside Victory*. It also meant that, in a very limited sense, she belonged to an aristocracy; she was meant to survive for the postwar period, provided that no torpedoes ripped out her guts, that no mines caved in her plates, that no shells or bombs smashed her superstructure into scrap; provided all that, she was a little less expendable than the bathtub hulls of the Liberties, a little more expendable than the C1s, the C2s and the C3s.

Her displacement was about ten thousand tons, her length something over four hundred feet. She had a forecastle deck, which gave her a graceful swoop up to the bow, and differentiated her immediately from the unbroken deck line of the Liberty. Amidships, she had a deck housing. Square, ugly, undifferentiated from the gray-painted metal of the rest of the ship, it climbed from the main deck in this fashion: boat deck, which housed the four lifeboats and gave the ship's officers a limited promenade; quarter-deck, bridge, topside and flag deck. One fat sack poked out of the housing, and four king posts surrounded it.

The gray ship was built for the belly of cargo she could carry, and every detail of her was a concession to cargo—no more. Five huge hatches opened to reveal that she was no more than a shell. The seven masts and king posts swung booms to load and unload her, and her own forest of booms, cable and rope made her capable of eating and then disgorging her own diet. Whatever comfort she held existed because cargo could not be disassociated from men, and her guns watched over that same cargo.

Her guns gave her a will of her own; expendable she was, but not defenseless. She had the power to strike, and to strike hard. Fore and aft were two gun tubs, raised platforms sheathed in half-inch steel plate. The forward gun was a seventy-milli-meter, quick, agile, able to swivel and snap like a swan's neck; aft, long, ugly, was a five-incher, able to fight a surfaced sub on equal terms, able to fling its shell six thousand feet into the air. Amidships, in six smaller tubs, were the twenty-millimeter machine guns, good for a curtain of lead when the dive bombers came in. She was not quarrelsome, the gray ship, but she could hit back if someone struck at her, and she could make her blow felt.

The guns were a navy affair, and under the five-incher was the gunners' forecastle, where eighteen navy men slept. Six more navy men slept forward.

As the purser said, the life of the gray ship was in her engines, oil-burning turbines which, when put to it, could turn over one hundred and five revolutions per minute and drive her at seventeen and a half knots. Turbines, boilers, fires and gener-ators were housed amidships, heart and guts, the bull's-eye for torpedoes, for shells and bombs.

Such was the gray ship, unlovely, stubby, confident, long of range, ready to go where orders took her.

About two hours after the purser's impatience, the gray ship cast off, and from slumber she came alive. From the midship housing aft, she trembled and purred; her plates vibrated; her propeller washed the dirty water, and the basin water washed back. The master, his patience tried the limit, demanded the pilot. In all his years, he'd never known a pilot to be on time, never; but the first officer, easy now, said, "He's on board, sir." "Then, mister, where is he? Is he drinking his tea? Is he sitting on the head? Or is he blowing his nose over the rail?" But at that moment the pilot came up the companionway, natty in his white suit, white shorts, white socks and shoes . . .

Below, on the gray ship, those who slept felt the change, the slight movement, the vibration, the waking up and coming alive, and they turned in their sleep, more easily than uneasily; in their sleep too they heard the hiss of the tugs, the chugging, the shouted orders, the second officer's repeat of the pilot's command, "Wheel amidships—" the blast of the whistle, the swirl of water, brown water which would presently become green and then blue water. The purser went back to his books, his nervousness gone. Two short whistles warned the change of watch, and the men coming off duty leaned on the rail and watched the harbor swing as they warped toward the canal. All over the basin, packed ships, merchantmen of all nations, patrol craft, destroyers, and menacing ships of war watched them. There were around the harbor the regrets men feel when they see another ship putting out to sea, the envy and the nostalgia. The gray ships, in time of war, have no proclaimed destination; somewhere, men wait for a ship; somewhere else a man knows where all ships are going and from whence they come; but he who sees the ship passing by knows only that it's outward bound . . .

The English pilot stood on the bridge and called his orders. London was in his voice, but he had been out here twenty-five years now. He went nowhere; for twenty-five years he had taken the ships in and out of the complex channel, released them from their brief, fretful imprisonment, and given them leeway for the ports of the world—San Francisco, Rio, New York, Antwerp, Saipan, Said—and then himself gone back; no ship liked his port, and sometimes it occurred to him, though he was not an imaginative man, that no ship liked any port. By now he went through his movements mechanically; you could roll back the water of the river, and it would not make much difference to him; he knew every mud hummock, every bar and channel. Always ahead of him was the thought, somewhat unclear, like the muddied waters of the channel, that he would take ship one of these days and go home; but he stayed on and the gray ships came and went.

Some of the men on the ship wrote letters, because the restless wonder of open sea again had to be expressed, and they would say things like ". . . my darling, we are going through the channel, and finally will be out to sea. So we should be home soon . . ." Or ". . . it was so hot here that it is good to be away . . ." But it could have been too cold as well as too hot; the core of the matter, on the gray ships, was movement. Logistics, the military called it, and on the gray ships movement expressed their purpose and their reason. Indeed there were a few men on the ship who never went ashore, in any port, as if the covenant to them was so dear that it couldn't be violated.

So the gray ship, which had slumbered, which had been dead to the purser, stinking dirty to the engineer, shirking to one, whorelike to another, came to life again and sailed out to the open sea. The gray ship was a stitch in a broad-woven pattern which had only slight variations in the whole of the warp and the woof. It sought little credit and found less. Though there was glory enough to go around, the gray ships did their job without glory; as their men wore no uniforms, so did they wear no medals.

They put out to sea again, and in a way that was its own reward. The brown water turned to green and the green water turned blue. The time-old phrase went the rounds of many lips, blue water, blue water, no bottom and a deep swell. The pilot shook hands all around, wished them good voyage, and climbed overside to his bobbing boat. On shore the blinker gave them clearance and wished them good voyage too. The captain, relaxed for the first time in many days, took his sharp turn on the quarter-deck, six paces port, six paces starboard, six paces port again. The messmen dumped the garbage overside, and the crows flew back to their own hot land. Full speed ahead came down to the engine room from the bridge, and given a lasting course finally, the helmsman fixed his eyes on the compass. Night fell and land dropped away, and in the brief, tropical twilight the gunners stood to general quarters. With darkness the ship blacked out and faded into the inky sea, and in the crew's mess three sweating A.B.s sat down for their evening of euchre.

Three Beautiful Things

MARK TRAVEN, THE writer, entered the Waldorf, looked around for a while, because he was five minutes early, and then went to the express elevators that go up to the tower apartments. He was wearing his best tweed, which meant the best of two, and he was a little excited at seeing Mr. Calwell, but not too excited, since he had no real hopes of anything lasting coming from it. Still, you could never tell, and it was with not a little pleasure that he told the elevator boy to take him up to the twenty-ninth floor.

"It's a nice day," said the elevator boy.

"It's a real fine day," said Traven. That was the way he felt. When the door of Mr. Calwell's suite opened, Traven entered with what he considered a fair mixture of humility and self-assurance. Miss Deale ushered him into the room. Miss Deale was about thirty, brunette, and very pretty; but with her good looks went an uncertainty that told people it was no picnic to work for Mr. Calwell. She and Traven had lunched the day before. Now she introduced Traven to Mr. Calwell, who waved the writer to a seat without rising.

Mr. Calwell sat with his back to the windows, and he motioned Traven to a deep chair facing him. He wore a dressing gown of green and red plaid and an ascot of the same material;

slacks, also of the same material, were matched by slippers of green and red plaid. On his fingers were a wedding ring and a signet ring with a large diamond. He was older than Traven had expected, at least sixty.

"This is Mark Traven, the writer." Miss Deale said.

"It is always a pleasure to meet talent," said Mr. Calwell.

Traven, who was rehearsing in his mind those of Mr. Calwell's pictures he had seen, so he could talk intelligently about them, nodded and said that he was very pleased to be there. It was his first interview with an important Hollywood producer, and it had so turned out that he was talking to just about the most important of the lot. He felt honored and said so.

"It is I who am honored," said Mr. Calwell. "Even if I am not always and continuously honored by talent—and for a man who don't respect talent I have no respect—I am honored by Thomas Jefferson."

"Thomas Jefferson?" Traven inquired.

"Thomas Jefferson," Mr. Calwell repeated, treating the name with both love and respect. "Of course, for Thomas Jefferson, you are younger than you should be."

"For Thomas Jefferson?" Traven said.

"But he himself was young, wasn't he?"

"Who?"

"Thomas Jefferson," Mr. Calwell smiled.

"I suppose so," Traven agreed, looking desperately at Miss Deale. But Miss Deale, who sat over on the other side of the enormous room, preserved a poker face.

"Of all the people in the world, you might say," Mr. Calwell explained, "who was there greater in the whole world than Thomas Jefferson?"

Traven shook his head, sparring for time.

"Washington? Lincoln? Theodore Roosevelt—not FDR,

you don't see FDR on a mountain in stone—but you don't compare them to Jefferson.''

"No, I guess not," Traven said.

"If I was talent and I had a choice, I would say to myself, go on writing about Jefferson.''

Traven swallowed and said, "I did a book about Paine, Mr. Calwell, my last book.''

"Who?''

"Tom Paine," Traven whispered. "Citizen Paine—''

"With Orson Welles," Mr. Calwell smiled. Then the smile vanished and he said, "That too is talent. Welles is talent if he doesn't break you. But he shouldn't mix in politics. That's the kiss of death, to mix in politics. That's why you're smart with Thomas Jefferson. Jefferson is not politics, he is immortality. You take a newspaper publisher and make a picture about him, that's politics. Orson Welles is talent; I admit that, and talent you got to respect. So I respect Welles.''

Traven nodded.

"Not like I respect Jefferson," Mr. Calwell added.

"No," Traven said. "Of course not.''

"But is there a place in Hollywood for Jefferson?" Mr. Calwell questioned seriously.

"I had hopes about Paine—" Traven began.

"You got a deal with Orson Wells?''

Traven shook his head, feeling like a blind man at the edge of a precipice.

"Then don't discuss him," Mr. Calwell said. "Even at Jefferson in short pants, people could laugh.''

"Sir?''

"With Bing Crosby, a costume piece is something else. I am not against laughter.''

"No, sir.''

"The world should be filled with laughter. But they shouldn't laugh at Thomas Jefferson."

"Yes, sir," Traven said. "But I'm afraid you have confused Jefferson with Paine."

"Welles confused him. Welles is talent, but if Welles comes to me and wants to work for nothing, I don't have him."

"That's Citizen Kane, sir," Traven said softly.

"But it's not Jefferson. First, I said to myself, if it's the last thing I do, if I lose a million dollars, I will make Thomas Jefferson. That's a public service; the whole world can look at America with Thomas Jefferson. But maybe the time isn't ripe. When I doubt a thing, even a little bit, I say to myself, the time isn't ripe."

"Yes, sir."

"Of course," Mr. Calwell added, "if it has three beautiful things, it will make money."

"Sir?"

"Mr. Traven, in all the world there are three beautiful things. Three beautiful things are immortality. You have three beautiful things and you will make money, even out of a public service."

"Yes, sir."

"Suppose I asked you to name three beautiful things?"

"Any three beautiful things?" Traven inquired uncertainly.

"No—no. You see, a talent is something. You got a talent for Thomas Jefferson. You should go on writing about Jefferson. That's a service. Can you write too much about Jefferson?"

"I don't know—"

"Your play is a service. Your play is something everyone in America should see."

"My play?" Traven asked.

"About Jefferson. Jefferson is immortality. But there are three beautiful things that are immortality in the box office. There is beautiful love. There is beautiful music. There is beautiful laughter. Those are three beautiful things. Those are sweetness. If you make a picture without them, even about Thomas Jefferson, what have you got?"

Traven shook his head.

"You got a public service, but not in the box office," Mr. Calwell said. He rose to indicate that the interview was over. "I'm happy to see you. Talent, I'm always happy to see. Talent is the most precious thing on earth. You shouldn't go to Hollywood and destroy your talent, Mr. Traven. You should go on writing about Jefferson."

When Mr. Calwell closed the door of his tower suite on Mark Traven, the writer, he turned to Miss Deale.

"I pay you three hundred a week to bring me lunatics," he said. "I pay you to waste my time."

"I'm sorry, Mr. Calwell," Miss Deale said. "I think you mixed him up with Sidney Kingsley."

"Who?"

"The man who wrote *The Patriots,* the play about Jefferson. Mr. Traven wrote about Tom Paine."

"I need Orson Welles like I need the measles. If you got to bring me talent, Miss Deale, you should only not bring me lunatics. Without that, I can live."

The First Rose of Summer

I WAS FOURTEEN when first love came to me, which was older
than some yet younger than others. A round and appropriate
age, you might say, and I was ignorant of ductless glands and
such things, but knew only the blaze of glory that poets have
always sung about.

At that time, my brother and I had a newspaper route,
which netted us fifteen dollars on good weeks and which we
both conducted after school. Before we were finished on this
particular day, my brother knew that childish things were behind me and that there were more than material reasons for
the deep and saintly sadness in which I had wrapped myself.

"What's eating you?" he asked me, and I told him about
it. It had been a gentle day, a sweet day. We delivered our
papers for the most part in five-story tenement houses, and my
brother's idea of equity was for me to take the top three floors
while he took the bottom two; being a year and a half older than
I and some sixty pounds heavier, he could enforce this edict,
but out of a basic concept of equal rights, I fought him on
every house. Today, however, I accepted. There was a flavor to
suffering; my whole heart was filled with music.

"I'm in love," I said.

"What?"

"In love," I said. "In love with a woman."

"No?"

"Yes," I said, with dignity that couldn't fail to impress him. "Deeply in love."

"When did this happen?" His respectful curiosity combined interest and a touch of admiration.

"Today."

"All at once?"

"Yes," I said. "I saw her in my English class, and I knew it."

"How could you know it?"

"The way I feel."

"You mean like taking the top three floors?" my brother asked hopefully.

"That's only a part of it. My own suffering is of no consequence any longer, because now I'm consecrated to something bigger than I am."

My brother nodded and watched me intently. "How *do* you feel?" he asked.

"Noble."

"Not sick?"

"Not with physical sickness. It isn't something I can explain to you."

"I guess not," he agreed. "What's her name?"

"Thelma Naille."

"Thelma?"

"Thelma," I repeated, savoring the sound of it, the joy of it, the inflection of it.

"You're sure?"

"Of course I'm sure."

"That's a strange name," my brother said. "She doesn't lisp or anything?"

"She has a voice like music."

"Oh. Does she know about this?"

"Naturally not," I said—almost sorry that I had taken him into my confidence at all. However, it was necessary. Being in love was going to complicate my life; that I realized from the very beginning, and I couldn't have become a cross-country runner without my brother knowing what the motivating forces were.

At that time, we both went to George Washington High School, which is at the upper end of Manhattan Island. School let out at three; we finished our newspaper route at six, and then, since we had no mother, we prepared supper, ate it with my father, who came home from work about seven, did our homework and turned in. Love alone threw new drains on my energy. With the cross-country running, only a holy devotion permitted me to operate . . .

My brother was waiting for me when I came out of the English class the next day.

"Which one?" he wanted to know, and I pointed her out.

"The tall one?"

"She's not so tall."

"She's five feet nine inches if she's an inch."

"Oh, no. No. Never. Anyway, I'm five feet eight myself."

"Five six," my brother said coldly.

"Not with heels. Anyway, the rate of growth is different in different people. I'm just hitting my stride. She's all finished. Growing, I mean."

"How do you know?"

"Well, how tall can a girl get?"

"If you can keep on growing, so can she. That's logical."

I conquered the chill of fear that stole over my heart. He was understandably bitter; I held no resentment against him; I was filled with an inner purity and I let some of it shine through.

"You look sick," my brother said. "I hope you're all right. She didn't even look at you."

"She doesn't know me."

"Well, why don't you introduce yourself?"

"I can't until I have some achievement to lay at her feet. I'm no one. Did you see how beautiful she is? Anyone would be in love with her. That's natural."

"I'm not in love with her," my brother said.

"Anyway—"

"What do you mean by laying an achievement at her feet?" my brother asked. "Are you going to buy something for her?"

I walked away. It was no use talking to him about this; it was no use talking to anyone. It was something I had to contain within me until I had won my struggle to make myself worthy. For a week I brooded about that. The football season was too far gone, and anyway I weighed only one fourteen, and football was a long-term project with all sorts of special skills required. Love, I was beginning to discover, was not something that stood still; it was a dynamic force that moved a person to immediate action, and when the week was over, I turned out for the track squad. After all, how many football players ever made an Olympic?

"Your feet are too big," the coach told me.

"For what?" I had gotten along very well with them until then.

"For sprinting."

"I don't suppose my feet will grow much more, and I intend to."

"We can't wait," the coach said.

"Don't you want to try me?" I pleaded.

"It's no use," the coach said patiently. "You can't sprint with such feet."

"Well, isn't there something where you don't have to sprint?"

"Your feet are against you. If you jumped, it would be just the same. Also, you're small and light—and that's bad for discus or shot. If you want to try for cross-country, you can."

"Cross-country?"

"That's right. You spend a year at that, and then maybe the rest of you will catch up with your feet. It's good training, if your heart is all right."

My heart was all right, and at three o'clock I was shivering in my underclothes in Van Cortlandt Park. It was a cold, bleak fall day, and a hundred other boys shivered with me. Then we started out, and for the next half hour, over hill and dale, we ran a course of two and a half miles. It may be that education, in probing the bypaths of knowledge, has discovered something crueler and more senseless than a cross-country run; if so, I missed it. I don't know what upheld the rest of the squad, but love carried me through pantingly to the end. I showered and joined my brother on the route, an hour and half late.

This time I couldn't make the top three floors, and I told him why.

"You mean you're going up there and run two and a half miles every afternoon?" he demanded.

"Yes."

"But why?"

"For her."

"You mean she asked you to do this?"

"How could she ask me when I've never spoken to her?"

"Who asked you then?"

"No one."

"You're crazy," my brother said, which was what I might have expected, his mind being capable of rising no higher above the dirt. For the rest of that week, there was a certain bitterness of feeling between us, something I sensed only vaguely, since all my acute perceptions were blurred by a fog of constant weariness. If ever in the history of western romance love was stretched to a breaking point, that was it, and it seems to me that it is a real tribute to the gentle passion that both my devotion and I survived. However, my survival was a tough-and-go business; if I did not walk in darkness, I certainly walked in a gray haze, and my classroom response became, if not downright idiotic, at least far from alert. More than before, I realized that I would have to become the best cross-country runner America had ever produced to redeem a faltering, tired, incoherent young man in the eyes of the woman I loved.

Somehow, the five weekdays passed, and without a complete loss of the saintly gentleness that was the most manifest outward indication of my passion. The cross I bore was made no lighter by my brother's grim curiosity; in a completely scientific manner, he experimented with my new tolerance. I came late to work, but I certainly did my share.

The paper we delivered was an afternoon paper, except on Sundays, when it came out in the morning. That meant we had to dig ourselves out of bed at 3 A.M., stagger over to the assembly room, and collate mountains of newsprint. By seven or seven-thirty in the morning, we were through with the delivery and could go home and catch a nap. Ordinarily, I would be tired enough, but the cross-country team—and whoever was the diabolical brain behind it—decided to hold a conditioning run on Saturday, five miles instead of two and a half; and when Sunday morning finally rolled around my accumulated fatigue was something to see. My brother's respect was tinged with awe by now, and there was almost a quality of gentleness in his suggestion that I go home and sleep most of the day.

"No," I said wistfully. "It would be nice, but I can't. I'm going to her house."

"You mean you've met her, you've talked to her? She invited you over?"

"Not exactly."

"You mean you're just going over and introduce yourself," my brother nodded admiringly.

"Not exactly that either. I'm just going to stand outside her house."

"Until she comes out?"

"Yes—yes, that's it," I agreed.

"Don't you think you ought to get some sleep first?" my brother suggested.

"I can't take the chance."

"What chance?"

I didn't try to explain, because there are some things you can't explain. Her house was a fourteen-story building on Riverside Drive. It awed me and overwhelmed me; it widened the gap; it made me search my memory for any evidence that America was a country where cross-country running was even nominally honored. And to make things more difficult, the house had two entrances, one on the Drive and one on the side street. There was no bench from which I could observe both entrances, so I had to take up my vigil on a windy street corner, reflecting morosely on the fact that even if the rest of me grew, I was not treating my feet in a manner calculated either to keep them at their present size or preserve them for sprinting.

There are cold places on earth; there are places that have a whole literature of coldness woven around them; they do not compare with a street corner on Riverside Drive on a cloudy

November morning. That is a special cold; a nice, wet, pene-
trating cold that increases slowly enough for you to perish with
a minimum of pain. By twelve o'clock I had finished with my
consecration to life and had newly consecrated myself to death.
There was a new poignancy to the realization that I would die
here like this, on her very doorstep—a communal one, true
enough, but hers too—and that she would not know. Yet
wouldn't she have to know? When she looked at my pale white
face, the ice rimming my lashes, wouldn't something tell her,
and wouldn't she regret that never by word or sign had she indicated anything to me?

It was about that time my brother appeared. He had a
brown bag under his arm. "I brought you some lunch," he
said.

"Thank you," I murmured. "It was sweet of you and good
of you to think of me, but food doesn't matter."

"What?"

"I didn't mean to hurt your feelings," I said gently.

"That's all right," my brother nodded. He was beginning
to realize that with love, you felt your way with an open mind.
"Try a salami sandwich. Suppose we go over to a bench and
sit down."

"No—we can't."

"Why not?"

"I have to watch both entrances, and you have to stand
here to see them."

"Won't she look for you when she comes out?"

I shook my head. "She doesn't know I'm here."

"What?"

"You keep saying *what*. I think you don't understand
what this means to me."

"No, I guess I don't."

"How could she know I'm here," I asked my brother, "when I never spoke to her?"

"Then what are you waiting here for?"

"For her to come out," I answered simply, eating the sandwich.

"And then?"

"Then I see her."

"But you see her every day, don't you?"

"Yes."

My brother looked at me searchingly. "Oh," he said.

"What do you mean by that?"

"Nothing. But suppose she doesn't come out?"

"She has to come out sooner or later."

"Why?" my brother demanded, parading the cold vista of logic. "On a day like this, she would be very smart to stay at home. She could stay at home and read the funnies. Maybe she's even got a party up there and all kinds of people are coming in to visit her."

"Stop that."

"I'm only trying to be logical," my brother said.

"You don't know how you're hurting me. If you knew, you wouldn't talk like that."

Indicating that if I thought so little of his advice, I could maintain my vigil alone, he left me to my meditations and to the incredible combination of damp wind that blew in two directions at the same time. The top of me wasn't so bad; I had a woolen cap and a short coat we used to call a Mackinaw; but my feet suffered. It was ironical to consider that it might be *her* fault that I would never be a sprinter; even the question of plain and simple walking began to raise doubts in my mind.

The sun had set behind the Palisades and the policeman on the beat was beginning to eye me uncertainly when my brother appeared again.

"Still no sign of her?" he said.

"I'm above anything you can say."

"All right. But Pop thinks you ought to come home."

"You didn't tell him?"

"Not exactly."

"How could you?"

"It's all right," my brother assured me.

"How could it be all right? How could a man Pop's age know what I'm going through? Even you can't understand it."

"I try to," my brother said. "Don't think I don't want you to be a great cross-country runner, because that wouldn't be true."

"You don't even understand that my only interest in this damned cross-country running is because I want to lay something at her feet."

"I just feel you ought to introduce yourself. Then if she were to come out while you're standing here, she'd know you. You got to admit that would be an advantage."

It was true; I had to. I turned it over in my mind until Wednesday of the following week, and then because it looked like rain practice in Van Cortlandt Park was cancelled. I took my heart in my hands and I stopped Thelma Naille when the dismissal bell rang. As I looked up at her, she was more than ever the Greek Goddess. I asked her how she went home.

"By bus."

"Do you go alone?"

"Sometimes," she said.

"Do you like to sit on the top—where it's open?"

"Sometimes," she said.

"Could I go home with you today?" I managed.

"If you want to," she said.

I walked on air. My heart beat like a trip hammer. Once, her hand even touched mine for just a moment. Outside, a northeaster blew, and I found a bus with an open top.

"It's cold up here," she said, when we sat down on the top of the bus. We had it to ourselves, the two of us alone with the whole world beneath us.

"You get used to it."

"And I think it's going to rain," she said.

"Maybe it won't, and anyway that's lucky for me because there's no cross-country practice."

"Oh," she said.

"That's like sprinting, only it goes on for two and a half miles."

"Oh," she said.

"I made the team," I said.

"Yes? Don't you think we ought to go downstairs?"

"You'll get used to it in no time. There are seventy men on the team, but that's the kind of a sport it is."

"Oh," she said. She turned up the collar of her coat and wrapped it more tightly around her. She stared straight ahead of her.

I made small talk to the best of my ability, but she didn't unbend, except to shiver occasionally. I even made one or two excursions into the matter of my feelings, and that was just as nonproductive of reaction. Then the sleet started, not much at first, actually not enough for you to really notice.

"I think we should go downstairs," she said.

"Oh, no. No. It's nice up here. Up here, you can see everything."

"Well, you did pay the fare," she said.

"That doesn't matter. I always pay the fare when I take someone on a bus."

"Aren't you cold?" she wanted to know.

"No. No—"

The sleet increased and then it turned to rain. For a minute or two more, she sat huddled against the rail. Then she stood up and walked to the back of the bus and down to the lower deck. I followed her, but I couldn't think of anything else to say until we came to her house.

"I'm soaked," she said. "I'm soaked through and through. And it's your fault."

"Just a little wet."

"No, I'm soaked," she said. "I'm good and soaked. Thank you for taking me home."

I told my brother about it later and he observed, "There you are. You can't tell."

"I love her more than ever," I said.

"Well—"

"What do you mean, well?"

"Nothing. Only tall girls don't like short men. That's something to think about too."

"I think it was mostly the rain. I guess she's delicate."

"She's awful big to be delicate."

"But she's sensitive," I said. "You wouldn't understand that."

She wasn't in school the next day, and I went through the tortures of the damned. "Call her up," my brother said.

"Call her?"

"Sure. Phone her. You know her address. Look up her number in the phone book and call her. She'll think it thoughtful of you."

I did as he said. A lady's voice answered. "Thelma is sick," the voice said coldly.

"Can I speak to her?"

"You can't," the voice said, and hung up.

I wouldn't want anyone to suffer the way I suffered those next few days. Penance was all I could think of. I had read in books about how people spent whole lifetimes atoning for some awful wrong they had done. I saw myself walking in her funeral. No one knew me, but no grief was like mine, because when all was said and done, I had slain her. I and no other. A lifetime would be hardly long enough to atone for that. I decided that I would do good things. My love would never change, never slacken; people would think of me as a saint, not knowing that in all truth I was a murderer. Even my cross-country running suffered. Instead of leading the pace, I lagged. The coach called me up for it, but what did cross-country mean now?

And then Monday came, and she appeared in school, and my heart sang again. She was paler—that was true—but it only increased her beauty. I went up to her and said:

"You were ill, and I'm sorry. If it was my fault—" I had thought the speech out very carefully, but she didn't permit me to complete it. Instead she broke in:

"You are a horrible, nasty little boy. Please don't speak to me again."

I skipped cross-country that day. I turned up for work at three and my brother shook his head somberly when he saw my face.

"What happened?" he demanded.

"The world ends, and you want to know what happened!"

"You'll still take the top floors, won't you?"

"Yes," I said sadly. "It doesn't matter. I still love her. I will always love her, I guess." I saw the future then, a grim and bitter man who turned his face from all women. They wouldn't know and neither would she.

Wake Up Glad

TULLY'S WIFE, A hard-working woman who looked older than she was, what with four children and the cooking and washing that go with them, could not speak of her husband for any length of time without referring to the fact that he woke up glad. If she put a heavy store in small pleasures and blew them up all out of proportion—well, that could not be held against her. Sometimes it tired the neighbors and the people in the stores where she shopped; but mostly they were used to reiterated observations, and, aside from the youngsters who were coming back from overseas, their horizons were limited.

She was fond of saying, "I like a man who wakes up glad. I like a cheery smile in the morning. I like a joke. I like the morning it should be what God made it for, the brightest part of the day."

That was the way Fred Tully woke up, and in the course of some years, she had repeated that information to everyone who would listen. She might have fastened on other things, but this took her fancy. She might have said of Fred Tully that he didn't drink as much as other men did in the part of Greenpoint where they lived. He went on a bender once in a while, but in the course of things he was a good, solid family man, a good provider, and rid of most of his wild ways as he passed the middle part of his thirties. He was good-looking, big-shouldered and tall, but a little stooped after seven years of sitting in a hack. He had once claimed a terrible temper, backed up by hamlike fists, but he never used his hands against his wife, and he would die before he would put a finger on one of the children.

Now a tire of fat around his belly took the edge off him, and when he rolled on the floor with the kids in the morning, making them late for school, he looked so much like a large, good-natured dog that his wife would say, "Now is that right for a man to be down on his stomach, wriggling like a beast?"

He woke up glad; he woke up singing. For him, the morning, the very early morning, was the best part of the day. The three boys and the girl would all pile into the bed, and he would roughhouse them over his wife's sleepy anger. He would whack them out of bed and into the bathroom. Once the priest had warned his wife that this sort of thing, a man and three boys and a girl, all half-naked, could lead to bad things, but Fred had said to her, "The hell with that—it only leads his fat head into his pants."

Fred put up the coffee himself. When he opened the can, he sniffed and sang. He sang as he measured the coffee. He sang crazy songs that he picked up from the characters in the garage, and no one had ever heard such songs in the neighborhood before, songs like, "Gimmick, gimmick, gimmick, gimmick—" and then with the kids joining in— "down to the bottom!"

Nobody in the whole house slept after the Tullys got up. There was no peace either, until he left with the kids, sometimes walking with them all the way to school. On the way, they sang; like characters, people in the neighborhood said. So when Tully's wife always came around to explaining that he woke up glad, it was in the way of an apology, too. Sometimes, she felt it would be more comfortable if Tully were like other people; sometimes, it even occurred to her that other people said stronger things about Tully. But she had been married to him a long time; she was used to him; and now that no more children came, God be praised, she sometimes found herself being in love with him like a schoolgirl.

Fred Tully knew that he woke up glad. He stayed glad, cheerful, easy, for about two or three hours after he got into his hack. Then it got him; every day it got him. It had been that way since the first day he went out, and he had been sitting in a hack for seven years now. By noon, usually, the morning was like a dream. Before he became a hack, he had worked in a dozen different places, mills, factories, warehouses. Twice he had driven a truck. But nothing like hacking; hacking he hated; he despised hacking. In the beginning, he would have given it up for any decent job; now, with the war over, he turned in about sixty a week, and you don't give up sixty a week no matter how you hate it.

By noon, this day, it was as bad as it ever was, always in midtown, heavy traffic, people in a resentful mood. Long ago, he had noticed how moods seem to run different, from day to day. "I wake up glad," he would tell himself, "I wake up glad, and by twelve o'clock, I'm like this."

He wanted a drink; when he wanted a drink that way, badly and savagely, in the middle of the day, he knew the storm signals were up; he knew it was hair trigger from here on. When he wanted a drink that way, he pulled in somewhere, had a sandwich and two or three cups of coffee, and kept his mouth shut. He kept his mouth shut in the lunchroom, and he kept his mouth shut for the rest of the afternoon. He went home, and the kids knew the way he was and left him alone. His wife knew the way he was, and thought to herself, "Well, he'll wake up glad. Let him get to bed now.''

Today, he had his coffee and a sandwich and got back into the cab; he never said a word. When some guys came in who knew him, and said, "Hey, Tully," he just nodded. When they got into an argument about the union and started in on the old refrain, "There's nothing in the world as dumb as a hack— there's nothing so low as a hack. In the whole world, everything's organized, but not the hacks. Go tell a hack something —tell him what's good for him. What about it, Tully?" he just nodded, finished his coffee and got out. He picked up fares and took them where they wanted to go. He had seven fares working downtown, and then a long one up to Eighty-second Street and Park Avenue. He didn't look at faces, continued to want a drink, and didn't answer when a customer tried to be pleasant. It was four o'clock when he turned east on Eighty-second Street and picked up a woman near the corner of Lexington.

When the woman got in, Tully just glanced at her. He had no center rear view in his cab, and it wasn't until later that he turned around to look at her. His first impression was just a dame in a good fur coat, yellow hair, and a polished face. The face was set and expressionless, and didn't tell anyone anything, and she gave him an address on Fortieth Street between Fifth and Sixth, grading the words in a flat, hard voice. He knew that kind of face and that kind of voice; as he started down Lexington, he took his lower lip between his teeth and held it there.

Traffic was heavy on Lexington; he made five blocks on the first light, only three on the second, and then the woman in back said to him, in that same, expressionless voice, "Why don't you stop squeezing nickels and turn up to Park?"

Tully turned west, and then downtown on Park. He felt little needles in his spine, and he hunched forward over the wheel. But it was slow on Park, too; it was one of those days when everything jams up, and it's slow all over the city.

"This is fine," his fare said. "This is fine. This is just fine."

Tully didn't answer.

"I adore cab drivers," she said.

The needles were jabbing at Tully now; they went in and out, cutting his flesh. At Forty-seventh Street, he turned west again. They jammed up in the line of cars waiting to spill out onto Madison and Fifth.

"You couldn't have done it better," the woman in back said.

Grinding his teeth over the flesh of his lower lip, Tully jerked the car into neutral and raced the motor. It was an old Packard, his cab, and the vibration of the motor promised to fling it apart. He didn't care; he wanted the motor to drop out onto the street. He'd walk away and leave it. Then the lights changed and the cars ahead pulled away. With horns shrieking, Tully moved to the corner and was caught there by another light.

"You planned that nicely," she said.

Tully put the car in neutral again. He turned slowly, knowing that the future was wild; here went everything. He looked at the woman and then he turned back. He tried to smile. What sense did it make? He brought home sixty dollars a week, and he woke up glad. And with all the kids getting out of the army, you couldn't go out and pick up a job around the corner.

But in his mind's eye was planted a picture of the woman. He had carried a thousand like her, and the mink was the same and the hair was the same, and the face, too; but it always flashed into his head, with insane regretfulness, that he'd never go to bed with a woman like that, like out of the window of Saks Fifth Avenue, he'd never touch one, he'd never get close enough to the face to know if you could get your fingernails under it and peel it off.

Then the light changed and he turned onto Madison.

"Why didn't you go across to Fifth?" she asked.

He noticed how his knuckles stood out, like white spots.

"I said, why don't you go to Fifth?"

"I figured Madison was better," Tully said softly.

"I'm late—can't you understand that?"

He was talking now; it was no use to try to stop talking. "Look, lady, I know my business. It's bad on all the avenues this time of day."

"I ought to take your number," she said.

"What the hell—" He put the car into gear and moved slowly down Madison.

"What did you say?"

He didn't answer; then he looked over his shoulder and saw that she had her purse open and was writing down his number.

"Don't do that," he said. He didn't glance back until the next light. She was completing the information from his card.

"Look, lady," he said. "It don't make sense to turn me in."

"Shut up and tend to your driving."

"That's what I'm doing, lady," he said evenly. "The cab ain't got wings."

The traffic started again, and Tully made two blocks before the light changed. In those two blocks, Tully thought of all the hacks who made a practice of recounting experiences with women like this one; but Tully never had any such experiences, and he always thought of the hacks as liars. In two blocks, underneath his fury, underneath the mounting rage that made him tremble, that made his gizzards and his bowels tremble, he couldn't get out of his mind the crazy fancy of a woman like this one telling him to take her somewhere, and then telling him to come upstairs to an apartment with her. He couldn't get it out of his mind, not even when the light turned and she said to him:

"You cheap chiseler."

He couldn't get it out of his mind as he deliberately opened the door of his cab, walked back to her, opened her door and called her some of the filthiest names he knew. As she screamed, flecks of the spittle blew in his face, but he still couldn't get the picture out of his mind. Not even when he saw the cop coming; it still sandwiched in between her angry screams, sandwiched in between the reflection that this was it, that all the time it was coming to a poor fat slob, whose only virtue was that he woke up happy in the morning.

The Police Spy

THIS IS THE tale of a police spy who became something other than a police spy, and his name was Bondar Shar. He was a young man, but you would not have thought so to look at him, what with circles under his eyes and the worries stamped on his brow. It was not alone due to the fact that he had a wife who was always ailing and five children who never had enough to eat, but also because he was the special police spy of Widee Shimer.

Widee Shimer was District Organizer for the Communist Party of India in the central are of the northwest; which meant that his territory stretched from the Sind in the west to the Punjab in the northwest, to Tibet to Nepal. In truth, a kingdom, and even an empire, as some might style it; but a Communist Party organizer in India being neither a king nor an emperor, Bondar Shar most often considered that central area to be an abomination, pure and simple.

For all of this immense area, Widee Shimer did not have an automobile; indeed, not even a tonga, not even a bullock cart, only his own two feet, and occasionally a ride on a train if he was going a real distance, like a hundred or two hundred miles. For the most part, he walked. Shimer was small and brown and wiry, and the skin on the bottom of his bare feet was tougher than leather. When he set out to go from one place to another, he moved at a sort of dogtrot that ate up a steady six miles an hour, even in the hot weather of the summertime, when the alcohol in the thermometer rises to one hundred thirty and even one hundred forty degrees. Down the dusty roads he would trot, with a cheerful good morning for everyone, for the bullock drivers whom he passed as if they were standing still, for the tonga drivers, whom he passed as if they were moving just a little, for the workers in the fields, for the water carriers, for the fat priests and for the skinny children, and for the young girls who smiled at him so shyly and sweetly.

And behind him came Bondar Shar, his police spy, cursing or growling or grumbling—and sometimes literally weeping with fatigue and rage. It is said that in other countries, where the rulers are rich and powerful and have money to burn, police spies work only eight hours a day, and panderers and informers even less. That may be; but in India, a police spy works the clock round. The rule is: for one Communist, one police spy. The resident police chief himself laid down the law. "After all," he said, "the empire is not what it used to be. If a bloody red can carry on, it seems to me a police spy should damn well be able to carry on, too."

So Bondar Shar carried on, sometimes weeping aloud with rage at the life he led and the calling he pursued. Sometimes, in desperation, when Widee Shimer set out on one of his journeys, Bondar Shar would hire a tonga, but the tonga driver would have to whip his little horse to keep up with Shimer, and sooner or later that led to an altercation between Bondar Shar and the driver. Often enough, hot words led to blows, and Bondar Shar would find himself in a fight while Widee Shimer trotted merrily away.

It was enough to depress a tougher man than Bondar Shar.

Every morning, he had to rise before it was light. Drugged with weariness, he would plod through the back alleys of Old Delhi, to the little shed outside and behind a bearer's hut, where Widee Shimer spread his pallet and slept. Slept, but did not live; as Bondar Shar would whimper to his wife, "The cursed man lives in a thousand places at once."

And Bondar Shar had to be there early, for at 5 A.M., as by the clock, Shimer would be up and going, off to party headquarters, where the red flag flew, or out into the countryside to a meeting of peasants, or deep into the rat race of Old Delhi to one of the printing depots.

It reached the limits of human endurance, and though some say otherwise, a police spy is human. It reached a point where Bondar Shar had to act, and for days he deliberated upon various courses of action. There were certain bad men in Old Delhi who did things for a price, but Bondar Shar was not certain that they would kill a Communist organizer; and, even if they were willing, where would he find the price? A killing is not a tonga ride; twenty rupees would be scarcely enough, and if word got out, the government might not approve. It was true that in the Punjab, when the government grew tired of a Communist organizer, they broke both of his legs and then tied him to a bed so that the bones knit crookedly, so that forever after one who saw a bearded Sikh waddling like a duck would recognize him for what he was; and it was also true that in Bengal they tore the fingernails out of Communist organizers and now and again cut off their thumbs. But right now the party was legal in the central area, and it might be a month or a year before it was illegal once more. And, being neither a yogi nor a fakir, the thought of a month or a year more of this drove Bondar Shar insane with despair. How many times did he say to himself, "Was ever a man so cursed?"

Still, he deliberated, considering this and setting that aside, until finally he arrived at the only practical thing a man might do. And, having arrived at a decision, he kept his peace, told neither his wife nor his cronies, but put it into action the very next morning.

It was still dark early that morning when Widee Shimer trotted out of the shed behind the bearer's hut on his way to work, pausing only a moment to nod good morning to the police spy. But that morning, Bondar Shar did not wait until Shimer had reached the approved thirty paces of space, and then proceed to follow; rather did Bondar Shar reach out and grasp the sleeve of Shimer's thin cotton shirt, telling him:

"Hold on there. Now wait a moment."

Wait a moment, indeed, Shimer thought, wondering whether a surprise move for the suppression of the party had been decided upon overnight, and what his chances were for knocking Bondar Shar over and tying him up with strips of his dhoti. But Bondar Shar had forced a more ingratiating smile than any police spy would have allowed himself if he were about to make an arrest.

"I thought we might talk," Bondar Shar added quickly. "Here we are, the two of us, going here and there and everywhere together, and yet never a word passes between us."

It was true, and Shimer was forced to acknowledge it. He did usually nod good morning and smile in recognition at other times, but never a word had been passed.

"But a police spy is a police spy," he said, choosing his words carefully and stifling any desire to indulge in invective.

"And a police spy is human," Bondar Shar returned.

"True," which was as far as Shimer would go; yet he found himself looking at the other, calculating his caste, which was probably Brahmin, his age, which could not be more than thirty, and his appearance, which was not uncomely, dark skin and clear brown eyes and good features, but woefully skinny, just as skinny as Shimer himself, and in that hungry land, there is a bond between skinny folk.

"Human," Bondar Shar repeated. "How many meetings have I sat through, listening to you speak and lead discussions, wedging myself in between walls, crawling on roofs and hanging onto windows? How many reports have I written? How many?"

"A good many, no doubt," Shimer said. "But I am already late, for there is an important conference at six o'clock. If you would walk along with me—"

"And if I should walk the prescribed thirty feet behind, we would have to shout. On the other hand, if I am seen speaking with you—"

"Who but bheesties and coolies will see us at this hour?" Shimer shrugged. "And who will they tell?"

Bondar Shar nodded in resignation, and plodded along at Shimer's side. "It is not that I listen without hearing," he said petulantly, still rubbing the sleep from his eyes. "You speak of the masses and of the people. You speak of the workers and of those who eat too little. You speak of how you must help the people, know the people, come close to them. You speak of a better life for the people. How many times have I heard that and written it in my report thus: *Widee Shimer assured the cotton workers that a better life can be won.*"

"Many times, I am sure," Shimer admitted.

"And what of me?" Bondar Shar demanded. "Am I not human?"

"You are a police spy, and even a police spy is human."

"True. But let me tell you, Widee Shimer, the life I live is not a life for a human being but for a dog. If I changed places with the lowliest coolie, I would be better off. Up before dawn to be here when you awake. Out to a peasant village, back to town. One, two, three meetings, one after another. A planning commission, where you whisper so low, I must invent words for my reports. A mass demonstration. A strike, where God knows whether my head will not be broken along with yours. Out to the villages again. Back. Into New Delhi, back to Old Delhi. Do you know how many miles you walk in one day?"

"A good deal, I suppose," Shimer said, a little uncomfortably.

"Twenty, thirty, forty miles in one day. Yes, only last week, forty miles in one day. And then meetings and conferences far into the night—until one and two in the morning. Do I see my children? Do I ever have a kind word from my wife? Better to be dead than a police spy in this miserable place. Yet what else do I know? For two years I studied to pass the examinations for the police. I am a civil servant, yet I would be happier as a water carrier."

Shimer's quick pace slowed. His small, bright eyes were narrowed, and he nodded his head. "You might be happier as a water carrier. I never thought of that. First you tell me you are human, and then you tell me you are unhappy. Yet you are a Brahmin, so you will not be a water carrier. Can you cook?"

"Worse than an Englishman," Bondar Shar said miserably.

"A shame. I always think, if worse comes to worse, a Brahmin can be a cook. Tell me, what do they pay you as a police spy?"

"Thirty rupees a month," Bondar Shar said.

Widee Shimer came to a stop and whistled softly. "Thirty rupees a month! Now, look here, I am a Communist organizer, alone, who needs no more than a bowl of rice and a pallet somewhere, and the money I am paid comes from the hands of workers and peasants, yet I am paid thirty-five rupees a month.

How can you live on thirty rupees a month?''

"I can't,'' Bondar Shar admitted. "Seven mouths to feed, and when have any of us had enough? When the children are sick, we can't call a doctor. Not even a pice for a sweet. Four years, my wife wears the same sari. In the winter, we shiver because there is no money for charcoal. In the summer we roast. If I were a police spy among the prostitutes, I would make a rupee here, a rupee there. If I were a police spy among the grain profiteers, my belly would never be empty, nor would the bellies of my children be empty. But to be a police spy on a Communist organizer—death would be better—I tell you, death would be better.''

"Death is never better,'' Shimer said softly. "Now I will tell you something. There are no quick cures for such deep-rooted cancers as the question of police spies. But we can make things a little better. We can make it possible for you to see your family now and then, to rest a little. By now, you know what generally goes on at our meetings. When I go into a meeting, you can go home. Then I will meet you later and give you a full report. And when I have a late meeting, you can go home to sleep. The next day I will help you with your report.''

Dubious at first, Bondar Shar finally accepted Shimer's suggestions. He came home, listened to his wife's scolding, and played for two hours with the children, especially Santha, the youngest, who was like a little doll cut out of weather-stained ivory. He did it once, and he did it again and again, and life became more bearable. And, in spite of himself, in spite of the fact that he knew it was wrong, that he knew it would lead to no good, he conceived a sort of affection for Widee Shimer. As a servant of the state, a civil servant, an officer of the crown, he knew that even to think such thoughts was rank treason. There was a table of wrongdoers, a ladder of crime, so

to speak. A petty thief was worse than a rice profiteer, and a
pimp was worse than a prostitute, and a murderer, of course,
was worse than any—but murderers and pimps did not have
police spies attached to them, and the Communists did. Actually, Bondar Shar was fairly well convinced that even to think
well of a Communist was tantamount to a crime. He tried to
remember that, when Widee Shimer asked him, some days
later:

"Is it true, Bondar Shar, that all police spies are paid as
badly as you?"

"Worse. I am a senior police spy. An apprentice police
spy earns twenty rupees a month. Of course, he would not be
attached to a person like yourself."

"Of course. In other words, you are exploited as badly as
the workers—with no recourse."

"How do you mean—no recourse?"

"I mean, you can't organize," Shimer said.

"Organize what?"

"A union. Let me point out to you—the tonga drivers have
a union, the cotton workers, the water carriers, even the bearers
and sweepers. In the strike of the cotton workers, we won them
four rupees a month advance. Even among the peasants, we are
building an organization. Do you know that in America, a
police spy works eight hours a day, not a minute more?"

"For what pay?" Bondar Shar asked cunningly.

"Twelve, fourteen hundred rupees a month," Shimer
shrugged. "Personally, I am not overly interested. Our work
is not for police spies—our work is for the people—"

He talked on, and Bondar Shar listened. For a whole hour,
Bondar Shar listened, and then he said to Shimer:

"If I were to bring a few other police spies, six or seven,
but personal friends of mine, you understand, could you find

time to talk to them?''

"I could find time," Shimer agreed.

But, thinking it over, Shimer wondered what he could say and what sense it would make. To Bose, the editor of the daily paper in the district, he said:

"What hope is there for a police spy?"

"The hope of death," Bose, a cheerful man, replied.

"Yet a police spy is human."

The little girl who read copy—she had seen three brothers die in the famine and a fourth in a British jail—interjected, "The question becomes one of form and content, my dear Shimer. The form is human, but the content is a yellow scum."

"I am a sympathetic man," Bose reflected. "But sympathy is not a bottomless well. Shall I feel sympathy for the cobra if I cut off its head?"

So Shimer held his peace, recalling the tremendous open-mouthed excitement of Bondar Shar, and the next day he went to the meeting at the appointed place, an abandoned clay pit where no one ever went, the foolish considering it to be haunted by the ghost of an angry holy man. But since neither Communists nor police spies believe in ghosts, it was considered to be an excellent place.

Not six or seven had Bondar Shar brought, but fully twenty, and Widee Shimer gazed most curiously at the varieties of men who squatted about. They were long and short, and in their faces were evil, avariciousness and hopelessness, too, cunning and bewilderment, but, common to all of them, a hunger that had never been satisfied, not even for a day, or for an hour. Looking at them, Shimer was filled with disgust and repulsion; he felt like that one in Rig-Veda who was made a confidant of snakes and crawling things, yet, the more he looked at them, the more certain he was that their hunger was not of the belly alone. He sighed, regretting that he had come here, and began to speak slowly, and laboriously. He spoke of many things, of the classes of men and of the oppressed and the oppressors, and ever as he spoke he watched the faces of the twenty accursed men in the clay pit.

"In this land," Shimer said—"aye, and within walking distance of this very place, stands the Taj, the most beautiful of all buildings on the face of the earth. It is like the blessed winter sunshine poured into a vessel of pearl and alabaster, yet what is it but a memorial to ten thousand slaves who built it, the beautiful tower of terrible suffering? How many tears are mixed with the mortar? The memory of slaves in a land of slaves—"

So he spoke, and an hour passed, and then another hour, and he came to the end of his words. Comrades he could not call them; he looked at them and they looked at him, and then Bondar Shar rose and said apologetically:

"Thank you, Widee Shimer. It is an honor to have the supervision of a man like yourself as my responsibility. Yet, before you came, we spoke among ourselves of other matters. We would form a union, so that our wages might grow and feed us."

The others nodded. There was a long, long moment of silence as Shimer weighed it in his mind, considering this side of it and that side of it, but finally he too nodded and told them:

"Very well. These and these are the things you must do to form a union of police spies."

So it was that Widee Shimer went away from the clay pit, troubled and puzzled, and the first union of police spies in India came into being. So it was too, that two weeks later, Widee Shimer arose in the morning, went out of his little shack, and discovered that a new police spy had been assigned to him.

"Where," he asked him, "is Bondar Shar?"

But the police spy said nothing.

"Is he sick? Has he been transferred? Or is there trouble in his family?" Widee Shimer demanded, a little annoyed with himself for being interested in the affairs of a police spy. But the new one said nothing; the new one only pursed his lips and narrowed his brows, as a police spy should.

Meanwhile, Bondar Shar sat in the office of the resident chief, who wore a white twill jacket, knee-length, white shorts, and beautiful white silk socks that came to just a few inches below the place where the shorts ended. The resident's cork helmet sat on his desk behind him; his knees were crossed, and he flicked at flies with a shiny black leather quirt. He was a most pleasant man, and he questioned Bondar Shar most pleasantly.

"You are a civil servant?"

And Bondar Shar said, "Yes—yes, indeed," not at all deceived by the pleasant manner, but terribly, terribly afraid.

"And you took an oath to support the crown?"

"Indeed," Bondar Shar agreed.

"Not just a civil servant," the resident said reflectively, "but a part of the secret service. His Majesty's most honored service. You realize that, of course?"

"Of course," Bondar Shar whispered.

"I discussed that with the commissioner. It troubles him. It troubles me, too. You understand?"

"Of course," Bondar Shar said, so sick, and yet just a little proud that he should have been the subject of discussion with the commissioner.

"We can't have organization within the service," the resident said sadly. "We can't have a union, you know. We shall want the names of everyone who was associated with it, you know. After you write down the names, I shall see that it doesn't go too hard with you.'' He pushed a sheet of white paper toward Bondar Shar.

''What names?'' Bondar Shar muttered. But he knew, and the resident knew that he knew. The resident had been a long time in India, and, as he put it, he knew the native, and Bondar Shar was very much of a native. So the two of them sat there and looked at each other, and the resident thought that some day the very devil would break loose in this land of four hundred and fifty million souls—although he admitted to himself privately neither that they were human nor that they had souls—and Bondar Shar, on the other hand, contemplated his own soul, its worth, its strength, and the madness that was running through him, through his fear and his terror, and prompting him to do a curious thing.

He shook his head, remembering his five children, his wife, his little girl in particular, the sweet, pungent smell of Old Delhi in the wintertime, the taste of a bheesty's bag in the summertime, and all the other good things men remember at such times.

''No?'' the resident asked softly.

''No, Sahib,'' Bondar Shar said, whispering, for he knew that terrible things would follow.

And then the resident did not argue or threaten, because he had been a long time in India.

First they pulled out Bondar Shar's nails. One by one, they pulled them out, and it hurt a great deal. At first, Bondar Shar cried like a baby, but in the end he was screaming like a woman in labor. Then they turned him over to the Gurkhas, because even though he screamed like a woman in labor, his screaming was sound and not the names of certain men. His screaming was prayers and oaths and pleas, and obscure things that only a police spy could think of, but never the names of certain men.

So they gave him to the Gurkhas and told the Gurkha staff sergeant in charge that what they wanted were some names. The Gurkhas did things to him. Little men from the hills, terrible men who know neither God nor honor, but only war and the use of their wicked knives. The Gurkhas did things that cannot be described. And when Bondar Shar was red all over and without consciousness, they went to the resident and said:

"He made many sounds, but not the names of men. Now he is dying. Never before was there such behavior on the part of a police spy, whom all men know to be cowards and swine. Only the poison of Communism can explain it."

"Then put him in a basket and bear him to his home!" the resident snapped, filled with disgust—since such things are not pleasant to white folk of gentle birth—and also with anger at the Gurkhas for going so far.

So they put him in a basket and bore him to his home, and presently there was a funeral, a little procession, true enough, for that is a land of many funerals, but a procession nonetheless, with four professional mourners, the wife and the children, and Widee Shimer.

A whole day Shimer spent, with the funeral and with the family, and then he came back to the little building in Old Delhi, where the red flag flies morning, noon and night.

"Where were you?" Bose asked him. "Are you an organizer or a gentleman of leisure?"

"Is there a girl at last?" the young lady who read proof inquired.

"Or did you decide you needed a vacation?" the trade-union secretary demanded.

"I walked in the procession of a cursed and despicable police spy, who became something other than a police spy,"

Shimer said quietly, and then, because in that land he who mourns the dead does nothing else, Widee Shimer turned to his work with the living.

Thirty Pieces of Silver

MY DEAR AND beloved Joseph:

It is some time now since the death of the Rabbi—of whom I have written before, as you know—yet I find myself deeply troubled by certain implications in your last letter. Are not men our concern, and should we not understand them? So that even so will He be blessed who fashioned man, not out of alabaster, but out of the good earth which gives us all other forms of living. I have always hated superstition—and the Rabbi did too, I might remind you—which is not needful to a good man, but to the evil and ignorant, the one to make with spells and incantations and the other to devour them. Therefore, should I not be disturbed, my good friend, when I find even you repeating this or that old wives' tale concerning the thirty pieces of silver—which were not thirty pieces at all, mind you, but a good deal more in many ways, as you shall see.

Money was concerned, by all means, and other things than money, too; but hindsight is no justification for this type of tolerance. Figuratively, thirty pieces of silver were paid; are they not always? Even when I was a child, the patriot Chaim ben David was sold over to the Romans to be crucified; and the village folk took thirty pieces of silver and laid it on the doorstep of him who had betrayed him. Thus a prophecy finds answer and proof in the hearts of the people, for their dreams do not change, nor their oppression; and one will always be found like this one, to make a sale of the living flesh and blood.

Nor did he hang himself, as it is already said; such men do not hang themselves; nor did the silver money paid as the price rot away. No, my friend, there is a stronger acid in that money, but it works slowly, slowly. Indeed, each piece of money has found its companions, and he—that unspeakable one—waxes well indeed. Yet a different kind of curse is visited upon him, as the Rabbi—blessed be his name—would understand, were he alive today; not the apparent miraculous devil, which the simple folk so readily conjure up, and which the Rabbi so patiently dismissed; but instead, a hatred of the act itself—a hatred that will some day root itself in the hearts of all people, so that even his memory will be cursed and thrice accursed.

Then, for the sake of the gentle Rabbi whom we both loved so well, let me tell you how it actually came about, some of which I witnessed and some of which I had firsthand from most trustworthy observers.

First the character of the man, the complexity that was indeed simplicity. Our beloved teacher knew this, and wherefor did he accept Iscariot, but for knowing he was not a bad man? Yet, what is good and bad, but the love that one man has for another and the degree of it; and when this small portion of love that he, Iscariot, was capable of turned to fear, the Rabbi took no action. From there on, Iscariot believed in nothing, for a positive belief is not separable from love. Fear is no substitute, for fear of evil can lead only to a compact with evil.

Iscariot was not a fool; neither was he a wise man; and all that was his own in the brief moment of his belief, he came quickly to despise, for there was no show and glitter to it. Shame, instead, led him to seek the approval of those he finally served, and then that became right, and the other wrong, and all morality departed.

Let me illustrate precisely what I mean. For the betrayal itself, he could have found a logic and a justification—as indeed he did, I am sure. When they entertained him, when they listened to him, when they flattered him, it was simple recourse to mock at all the Rabbi taught, to laugh at all the Rabbi preached, to slander all the Rabbi promised. I was not a blind follower of the Rabbi, but I understood the sweet humility of him and the almost incomprehensible goodness of his soul, yet I myself know how easily that could be turned into its opposite with just the cheapest, easiest kind of cynicism. To do so was no great feat on the part of Iscariot, but why did it not halt there? In a sense, that is the key to this discussion of ours.

You know that they were coming to Jerusalem, and Pilate conferred with the elders, with those wealthy and shameless ones, so that it might all be done quietly. For, make no mistake, he fears us; with all of his legions, his might and power, he fears that wild Jewish flame that flares so quickly and so hotly. Do it quietly, he said; and that was the word they passed on to this creature. And he answered them, saying, not with a blow but with a kiss.

And, indeed, that is how it came about—that when the Rabbi and his followers came close, Iscariot went to them. I was not there, but from one who was I had it that the Rabbi looked at him, and that was such a long, searching look that another would have melted. But when love is gone, where is pity; and when honor had departed, where is truth?

Now you come to greet me, my child—is what the Rabbi said, smiling that curious smile of his, which you remember so well, I am sure; and then, without answering or speaking a word, Judas Iscariot kissed him full upon the lips, marking him, so that they were able to take him.

That same day, I saw this unspeakable person myself, and it is not true that he was noticeably disturbed. If anything, he wore an expression of pious assurance, and I heard a woman remark that in him the spirit was hardly concealed by the flesh. As time passed, this changed to a sort of patient resignation, filled with righteousness, a silent acceptance of some unspoken sorrow. But in conjunction with that, you must understand, there were new clothes, new slaves, new living quarters, an amazing variety of perfumes and women—so that while the soul exudes patient suffering, the flesh does very well indeed.

Whence rose the legend that he had slain himself, I am at a loss to know; that I must place with the thirty pieces of silver. If they were thirty, then the true miracle is how they have grown, for already Iscariot owned four ships, a house on the hill, and seventeen slaves. He does a very brisk business in slaves, Jewish as well as gentile, and he employs six people in his countinghouse.

Just the other night, Pilate gave a banquet for him; for he has relieved Pilate of the embarrassment of Claudia, for which the Roman is inordinately grateful. This was Iscariot's first appearance in more than a week, since he underwent a very painful operation to remove the signs of circumcision; and it was said that the spiritual qualities in him were intensified, as well they might be now that he is a Roman citizen. It is also accepted that he will marry Claudia.

I saw him myself earlier today. I was walking along the street as his litter approached, borne by four well-groomed slaves. I naturally would have passed by, but he stopped the litter and barred my way. You too? he said to me, and when I made no answer, he went on to say, You cannot understand, can you? You can only hate. At least I no longer hate. I no longer live in a world where everything is black or white.

All this he said in rather bad Latin; and, listening to him, I seemed to gather more of the nodule of the Rabbi's preaching than ever before, for I understood that Iscariot himself was no more than the evil odor that arises from any pool of corruption, and that he is a shortsighted man, indeed, who sees only the miasma and not the source. For him, then, at that moment, I had neither love nor hatred, admiration nor condemnation, fear nor trust. Quite coolly and detachedly, I looked at him, at the whole measure of the man, and then I went on my way.

Did I say he was not unhappy? He is not, I think; but happiness and unhappiness, in our terms, are as closed to him as color is to the blind. He has shaved off his beard, and his face is round and sleek. He has put on a good deal of weight, and in his Roman clothes, until he speaks, he might well be taken for a successful citizen. Soon he will leave for Rome, making proper provision here for his interests, and will take up residence there. It is also rumored that he plans to write a true account of the Rabbi and of the movement the Rabbi led, and it is surprising how readily it is accepted that this one is well fitted to speak of the man he sold.

What his other pretensions are, I do not know, nor do I particularly care. To write of him is not a pleasant experience, but it is necessary—even as constant and unprejudiced curiosity is the basic requirement of any student of people.

Forgive me for being so lengthy; but recognize, too, that a supernatural interpretation of a most understandable procedure can hardly do honor to the name of our beloved teacher. Far better that all should know the whole truth of this shameful creature, so that we may approach a time when the weakest of men will not be driven, by their own fear, to drag all that is godly in them through the filth. . . .